- - - - - - - - -

The

Imposition

of

Unnecessary

Obstacles

Also by
MALKA OLDER

MALKA OLDER

The

Imposition

of

Unnecessary

Obstacles

Tor Publishing Group
New York

THE IMPOSITION OF UNNECESSARY OBSTACLES

A Tordotcom Book
Published by Tom Doherty Associates / Tor Publishing Group
120 Broadway
New York, NY 10271

www.tor.com

Tor® is a registered trademark of Macmillan Publishing Group, LLC.

The Library of Congress Cataloging-in-Publication Data
is available upon request.

ISBN 978-1-250-90679-3 (hardcover)
ISBN 978-1-250-90680-9 (ebook)

Our books may be purchased in bulk for promotional, educational, or business use. Please contact your local bookseller or the Macmillan Corporate and Premium Sales Department at 1-800-221-7945, extension 5442, or by email at MacmillanSpecialMarkets@macmillan.com.

First Edition: 2024

Printed in the United States of America

0 9 8 7 6 5 4 3 2 1

For my mother, Dora Vázquez Older,
whose careful and appreciative first readings
encourage me through every book,
chapter by chapter.

There are other ways to live.

The

Imposition

of

Unnecessary

Obstacles

Prologue

People went missing on Giant.

People stumbled or jumped or were pushed through at-moshields and fell off platforms. They took dares to walk a portion of ring between platforms and lost their balance even if they remembered not to asphyxiate. The entire planet yawned there, an endless gaseous void into which bodies disappeared irrevocably.

Mossa was not alone in the railcar; transport on the route between Sembla and Valdegeld was (as Mossa had cause to know) frequent and brief enough that there had been no reason to vouchsafe her use of the Investigators' private railcar. She was sharing a carriage with three chattering students and an older person, perhaps with some business at the university or perhaps destined for another platform farther along the ring, and so she was careful not to move her lips as she thought through this explanation, or report. It was a habit long ago developed out of practice, or loneliness: reciting what she wanted to say to some imagined other person, aloud or internally. That way she would be ready when she had someone to explain it to; but it also helped her to organize her thoughts. Or perhaps, at this point, she couldn't refrain from involuntary narrative, and learning to do it silently at least gave her an outlet for discourses that others found boring.

As in this case. At least, she expected that none of the people around her were interested that *A startling percentage of cases brought to the Investigators dealt with missing persons. It might even be considered the raison d'être of the service, if you looked back at the historical case that led to its establishment, not long after Giant was settled. After the controlled, condensed environments of the spaceships and stations, where everyone was within contact all the time, life on a planet with a dense, communications-unfriendly atmosphere seemed full of gaps and mystery. Particularly in the rapid expansion period, people would disappear into the growing network of platforms and rings, and there would be no way to know whether they were prospering or vaporized unless someone went to find out. The Investigators were also something of a reaction against the hierarchical ethos of the space stations, a community service that was not about crime or castigation but about resolving some of the lacunae in communications across the foggy planet.*

Of course, they evolved.

Disappearance, too, took on new cultural significance in this context. There were persistent rail tales, renewed mu-

tatis mutandis in every generation, about remote platforms where the one person nobody could tolerate was required to step off into the murk, or told to leave and jumped instead. The stories usually drew some lesson from it—sometimes the communities never recovered, sometimes the drastic step solved all their problems—but of the two verified cases of this happening that Mossa was personally aware of, no follow-up had been done to learn the aftermath.

Mossa kept her eyes fixed on the view from the railcar window, the constant motion of the subtly colored vapors overlaid with the faint reflection of the people in the car. She was reciting this explanation, she knew, because she wanted to distract herself. Or perhaps because she could think of the person she would like to explain it to, but wasn't sure she should.

A lonely practice; a practical loneliness.

Not all of the corpses disappeared into the planet. Bodies were thrown into furnaces or composted into much-needed growth medium. And not all of the missing persons had died. Some were found on another platform where no one had expected them to be, or drunk or high under their bed or someone else's, or transformed in some way or another and pursuing a new life under another name.

And some of them were never found.

Most of them were never found.

Exiting Valdegeld's main station, Mossa felt the route to Pleiti's rooms tugging at her as though it were illuminated on her mind-map of the platform. She shook her head at herself. Pleiti probably wasn't even there: she would be in her office, poring over her data and calculations as an eco-system extinct for centuries repopulated in her imagination. The thought summoned an image of Pleiti coracled among her cushions, entirely ensconced in the workings of her mind. Mossa had never loved being ignored as much as when it allowed her to observe Pleiti abstracted.

Later. Mossa started down Supal, then took the turn toward the Speculative campus. For now, she was in Valdegeld to investigate a missing student. Perhaps, after . . . perhaps if she searched long enough, it would plausibly be too late to go home.

In the image in her mind, Pleiti raised her head from her work, looked at her, and smiled.

Mossa smiled back, baring her teeth into the cold wind blowing down Weilo Road. Perhaps Pleiti would welcome her without the excuse. Perhaps she wouldn't be asking too much, or promising more.

Perhaps, tonight at least, she didn't need to work *that* late.

Chapter 1

It was the sort of lecture I liked: a topic that I knew enough about to follow easily, but little enough about to feel like I was learning. Although it was a Modernist scholar speaking on what was, technically, a Modernist topic—the literature of alienation over the past two and a half centuries—it was closely enough linked to Classics via an explicit comparison to writing from the last decades of life on Earth that it had been allocated one of my favorite lecture halls in the Classical faculty. The seats were warmed, the glass covers on the gas lamps were an ancient and kindly yellow, and a tea service, authentically brought from Earth generations ago, shone on a sideboard amid chafing dishes and covered trays, promising cheering refreshment.

And yet I was having difficulty maintaining my concentration. My mind drifted like fog: from the delicate wordplay of Zint Plistor; to the system of gas-piping keeping the cushions toasty; to the net of rails girdling this permeable planet; to the latest species micro-map I had populated for my own research, tiny dots like a cross-stitch, satisfying to complete yet ultimately useless; to (with an effort of pouring myself back into the present) the erudite punning of Candela Roon, whose work spanned the Transition; to the precise varieties of dainties likely to be lurking in the tiered trays by the teapot; to the words of a dead man who had accused me and mine of excessive comfort.

Annoyed—with myself as much as with the dead—I glanced at the wall, where a crafted, cog-bound timepiece detailed the progress of no less than seven Classical calendars and mechanically demonstrated the placement of sunlight on a rotating model of Earth; a small dial in the lower corner indicated the local time on Giant. Not much longer now. I dragged my mind back to the lecture; meditated on the anachronisms of the tea service design; then moved on to (a leap, but the thought, like the dainties, had been lurking for some time) the probabilities of my seeing Mossa that night (slim) or any night before I chose to betake myself to Sembla on Earthday eve (not much broader). I was still meditating on that concern, with a curl of fancy into how that meeting, should it happen, might unfold, when the lecture ended.

Still somewhat dazed with my warm imaginings, and more relieved than I would have liked to be that the talk was over, I gathered my (largely unused) bloc into my satchel and made for the tea table. There were the tomato chutney tarts I was fond of from previous talks at this hall, and lovely little custard wagons. I had not tried the latter before, and discovered, unsurprisingly but to the detriment of my atmoshawl, that they cracked unpredictably and had a tendency to drip.

"Pleiti!" I turned from my cleanup efforts to see Gartine, another scholar, approaching. "We don't often see you at these Modernist events."

"I find different perspectives can be refreshing to the mind even if they are not directly useful." Remembering that Gartine's research group had been one of the sponsors for this talk, I attempted to pivot from *professionally modest* to *effusive*. "Naturally, this particular talk offered much . . . the speakers, so well chosen . . ."

"Mmm. Well, I'm pleased to see you so little affected by recent events," Gartine went on, meaning exactly the opposite.

"Not nearly as eventful as the chisme made them seem." It was my standard reply, honed over the months since I had become notorious at the university, but I had to swallow an unexpected wash of bile. "Really, I had very little to do with it." Gartine believed me no more than my other colleagues, and seemed disinclined to give up, so I did instead. *Weariness,* I self-diagnosed, and made my excuses, hoping it didn't look like flight.

The chill revived me somewhat as I stepped from the salle. The sky was lightening; events like this one tended to span the dawn, so that people finishing their diurnal could stay up a little late, while those on the other schedule could wake a little early. I was in the former group, on this occasion, and my steps thudded wearily on the platform, exhaustion a gravity multiplier as the sun started its race across the sky.

The tradition of divided schedules, with some of the population sleeping while the other was active, had started in the early days of settlement; or, strictly speaking, before then, on the spaceships, but it was on the settlement that it had taken its current form. There hadn't been enough places to sleep, early on; not just beds, but places offering sufficient warmth for a person to safely lie still through the night. Even after they built the first atmoshield—not something we would recognize as one today, not even really worthy of the name, as it was an impermeable dome more like a ship's hull—that first platform was crowded and precarious.

What was stranger was that the practice had stuck, even after the settlement had expanded and inhabitants were able to live in approximately Classical ways, with work and agricultural cultivation and sleep and family and, eventually, leisure and hobbies and elite centers of learning. Of course (I thought, as I continued my walk, well wrapped against the cold, the early sun barely tipping over Valdegeld's august buildings into its narrow streets), of course all those activities had been constrained at first as well: not enough university space to give classes to everyone who wanted them at once, the agricultural rhythms made possible by satellite mirrors requiring extensive working hours, and so on. But I liked to believe there was a tendency towards flexibility as well, a willingness to shuffle circadian strictures in the new environment of Giant. Why, I knew people who worked on a night-day pattern instead of day-night—Sintra, for example, in Classical geography, claimed she liked it because she could easily meet up with people from both the more usual schedule groups.

I was, by this point, nearly to my rooms, on Thanma Street. I considered stopping at the tiny poultry farm on the next corner for breakfast, but decided I would rather reach my rooms sooner, indulge in a warm bath while the tea steeped, and then work in a desultory, pleasant way on my new project for a little while before I went to sleep.

My rooms are in a narrow, four-story building reserved for scholars in Classics, nearly two hundred years old and exactly what people imagine when Valdegeld is mentioned: metal walls beaten into the textured, herpentine patterns popular during the era when much of the university's physical plant was built; quaint windows designed to hold extra layers of atmoshield, although now, with the exception of those on the top floor right which are original, they have all been replaced; an arching entranceway; and, of course, the porter's lodge just inside the door. At that hour I was a little surprised not to see the porter on duty sitting at the reception station outside the lodge, so I knocked quickly on the open door and poked my head in for a greeting.

"Ah, there she is," said Genja, a solidly built woman with a long meta-braid down her back. "I told you we wouldn't miss her."

"And right you were," responded Mossa, uncurling from the chair opposite her. "It's been a pleasure sitting with you indeed."

"And you. Have a good day then—or evening, as may be," Genja added, quirking her head at me as Mossa joined me at the door.

"You could have come up, you know," I said over my shoulder, as Mossa followed me up the stairs. It was a by-product of having live-in oddsbodies around the place that they were aware of visitors and, unless they tried very hard not to pay attention, who stayed the night. Mossa had never seemed particularly shy of people noticing our relationship, but she might have been unsure of my feelings on the matter.

"Thank you, but in this case it was no bother," Mossa said, her voice soft as we passed the doors on the first level. "I was feeling sociable." I glanced back with some skepticism; Mossa would not often be described as *sociable.* But her mien was entirely serious, and I reflected that, while she was not one to speak for the sake of speaking or enjoy crowded conversation, I had noticed her particularly engaging in discourse those people that most scholars would exchange no more than pleasantries with. I was, as I opened the door, feeling rather relieved that I *had* chosen to look in on the porter's lodge.

"Tea?" I inquired, unwinding myself from my outdoor accoutrements.

"If you don't mind," Mossa said, watching as I raised the fire. "I stopped in without warning, and you are probably tired after a long day . . ."

"I'm happy to see you," I said, almost managing not to hesitate before I pressed a kiss to her lips, and then continuing on to put in an order for the scones I knew she was partial to. "Are you . . ." I almost asked if she was staying, meaning more: *Are you coming to bed with me now, immediately after tea, or will you talk and then leave?* Surely not though, in general we kept the same schedule, and why would she arrive at this hour if not to—

My steps stuttered to a halt; I turned to her. "You're here on work."

Mossa did not flinch. "Not here in your rooms, but yes, here in Valdegeld."

I had intended to lounge beside her on the cushions, but fell into the low chair instead. "Is it—" I didn't know what to ask. She was an Investigator, obviously it was a poor prospect for *someone*. What I wanted to know was *Is it like last time?* Would it upend my life, shake my faith in this university, make me question my entire life's work?

Would it throw us together, like the last time Mossa came to my rooms on work, or would it unstitch us?

Mossa shrugged a little, perhaps as a response to my uncertainty, perhaps settling herself on the cushions. "A student is missing. I have only just started looking into it, but you know. People go missing here. They stumble or jump or get pushed through atmoshields." She paused abruptly. "It's . . ." I wondered if she too was trying to find a way to say *Not like last time,* without knowing precisely what quality we were both hoping to avoid. "It may be bad, but this early on there's nothing to say the student won't turn up in a few days after an impromptu holiday somewhere."

The dumbwaiter dinged, and I rocked forward to go for the scones, but Mossa was on her feet first.

"You've had a long day, I can tell." She let her fingertips glide over my temple, my cheek. "Relax, bathe, or change if you like. Or were you going to bed?"

I hesitated again, but this time from a delicious sense of choice rather than uncertainty. "A lave, and then I'll rejoin you."

I emerged from the bath feeling far more balanced on my axis. I had wrapped myself in a quilted dressing gown, partly in hopes of being unwrapped thereof, partly as a signal that I was indeed relaxed and comfortable, not standing on ceremony with my paramour—a signal as much to myself as to her. She was sprawled across the cushions before the fire, clearly relaxed (or exhausted?) herself, which made it easier to slip down to join her, plucking a ginger and pear scone as I did.

"Do you want to tell me?" I asked, leaning into her lithe solidity, her warmth by my side and the fire warm before us.

Mossa turned her head sharply in a half shake. "I don't mind but . . . so far at least, it's not so interesting." Not like last time. I exhaled. "I'd rather talk about your research." I settled into a further recline, and she slid her fingertips into my hair. "How is your latest matrix coming?"

"Oh, the usual," I said with a yawn. "I'm early on in this one," I added, to excuse the lack of urgency.

"Are you moving to another area of research?"

"Hmm?" I swallowed the crumbles of scone in my mouth. "No, why do you ask?"

"That book, on the writing desk? It's not in your usual topic."

I turned to look, even though I already knew: like all the books from the library, the metal casing of the chip was unadorned with illustration or even a title. "How do you know that?"

She waved at the chip. "The library number. All your books start with 067, sometimes 068 or 9. This is 043."

I had to breathe deeply through it: the sudden inrush of warmth that Mossa had poured that much attention into the details of my life; then the downswing of recalling that such details, for her, were as easily imprinted as a Classical quotation for me. "Yes. It's a new project, in fact, though more a sideline than any change in my primary research area, a bit of a lark."

I said it with a twitch of defensiveness. It was not so long ago that Mossa had suggested I revolutionize the way Classical scholarship was conducted, find a way to research potential ecosystems for the reseeding of Earth without depending on attempts to exhaustively mimic the balance of what had lived there before humans crushed it. I had pondered quite a bit what such a new form of theorizing might look like, was still pondering intermittently. But the cataclysm Mossa and I had been involved in, though it had reordered some of my ideas, had not erased my responsibilities at the university; if anything, it had increased them, as I was pulled into the strong and often conflicting currents of reaction. It had been far easier—and, if I was honest, comforting—to slide into my old patterns of research. I had been rather expecting Mossa to note that fact with some gentle critique. I had not fully given up on change, but this particular project, exciting though it might be in the moment, was anything but revolutionary.

I took a sip of tea, but she was regarding me with apparent interest, so I went on. "The university received a soil donation from Cater Rallon, the ag magnate. They've decided to use it in the Soyal Courtyard—you know, by the Silvered Library?—to turn it into a small park, and they want to grow a garden based on an example described in Classical literature."

"And they want you to interpret the literature to design it? That's marvelous!"

"Well, as one of a small squadron." As the leader, in fact, but she would deduce that soon enough so there was, literally, no need to boast. "It's exciting actually—to be doing something that will see an immediate effect, a change in the environment here . . ." As opposed to endless efforts to find the perfect combination of species to repopulate Earth, but that was the ramp onto a thought-spiral I'd had quite enough of lately—"And it's rather refreshing to be reading outside of my usually narrow range."

"Time or location?" Mossa asked, taking another scone and dusting it liberally with cocoa and cinnamon powder, followed by a pinch of garam masala.

"Both, although not terribly far in either direction. The end of the previous century, and in Canada rather than England. We've found a wonderfully specific and complete description of a garden—I'm just reading through the rest of the novel to see if there might be any additions later—it doesn't have the plan, of course, but the number of floral species mentioned is, is, it's fantastic really." For all my enthusiasm, I ended with a sigh, and we were silent for a while but for the quiet rushing of the fire.

"I'll look forward to walking through it," Mossa said at last, and as I wondered whether there was an unspoken *with you,* her sly smile reminded me of our walks in the gardens of Sembla, where she had kissed me for the first time since our tumultuous relationship as students. So I leaned towards her until it happened again.

Chapter 2

I did not have a tutorial to give the next morning, nor any meetings, and while I was dimly aware of Mossa rousing herself from the bed we had shared, I'm afraid I felt no obligation to rise myself until it was time to see her off. I believe I even mumbled something to the effect of "wake me before you leave," but it may not have been intelligible. She did wake me, however, leaning over fully dressed and gripping my bare shoulder as she repeated my name until I drifted into consciousness.

"Sorry," I said, grasping at reality. "Are you leaving? Let me just find my robe—"

"It's not that," she said, with too much gentleness. "There was a message for you. They've found the body."

"Not your missing student?" I asked, fully awake at last. "I'm so sorry—" And I had distracted her last night, when she could have been out looking—but no, that was foolish, Mossa never would have let herself be distracted from such a duty, she would only have come once there was no more to be done—

"Not the student," she said, still over-sweet, and pressed a mug of tea into my hands. "The rector."

When I had thought, during the lecture the night before, that I was overly attached to the words of a dead man, the *dead* part was an assumption, almost a metaphor. Rector Spandal had taken his stolen biomaterials and launched himself Earthward; his chances of survival were, by any reputable estimate, minuscule, and even if he survived he had certainly left the mortal plane of Giant and its moons, and he would not be back.

A corpse, unexpectedly, was another level of finality. One of the principles gleaned from the end of the world, now enshrined at the Sunken Memorial in Yaste, was that humans will believe in completely unrealistic probabilities to their detriment. It seemed I had not moved beyond that propensity.

It wasn't that I had wanted the rector to survive, particularly. In those last minutes on the launchpad I had seen his monstrous selfishness, beyond the damage he had almost certainly done to our efforts to return to Earth. Even so, the reality of his death (In the landing? From environmental toxins? A failure of survival efforts?) felt like a depressingly damp thud to close out the episode.

I took some grim satisfaction over my lonely breakfast (Mossa did have to get out on the track of her missing student, though she left me well cosseted when she went) in the quandary this would offer the university. (And how sad, that I should be enjoying in any small way the discomfiture of this institution that I had loved, learned from, and pledged my career to!)

After the events leading to Spandal's self-ejection from the planet, the university's first, foolish reaction had been an attempt to fog over, not to say completely obviate, the erstwhile rector's perfidy. Mossa and I had chuckled, by the fire in her neat rooms in Sembla, over the certain doom of that approach. After all, dealing with the trajectory of the (figurative) railcar the rector had set in motion incurred the launches of not one but two extraorbital spacecraft and could hardly go unnoticed. The powers that remained at Valdegeld, post the rector's hasty and dramatic exit, had eventually admitted to an extremely muted version of the rector's misdeeds (indeed, I was not entirely sure that they had ever made public the murder). They never mentioned my name, but faculty gossip got ahold of it all the same, lending a bitter irony to that memory of snickering with Mossa about media strategy.

There had been a lull of several months while the rector's illicit ark traveled to Earth and the probe that had been launched soon after (but not soon enough) followed. Even then, the probe had orbited for some time before it could even confirm that the rocket had managed to land on Earth; it had subsequently spent some time collecting data, and that data further had to be transmitted back to

Giant and analyzed. I still had no idea what evidence they had found of the rector's demise: I didn't think fragments of the rocket would be enough, so presumably images of his corpse . . .

I put down my tea abruptly. Time to get to work.

I spent the daylight hours, or what was left of them, continuing the population of my latest matrix: reading an account from mid-twentieth-century England, teasing out any reference to animal and plant species and attempting to determine as finely as possible their location and ecological relationships, and using that data to construct a mapping matrix. Normally I could lose myself in at least one part of my work, whether the close reading or the calculations or the minute changes in the map with every entry; unsurprisingly, none of that was holding my interest. If I wasn't thinking about the rector or his end, I was wondering how Mossa's search was going and, with a faint queasiness, what had happened to the missing student.

Around dusk I broke for a quick meal of lentil stew and decided that I had reason enough to knock off early and switch to the garden project for the rest of the day. It was an immediate lessening of drag, a feeling of ease and eagerness as I delved into the list of florae, cross-referencing with pictorial references, considering the size of the courtyard and sketching a possible layout for the garden. At some point the fog of my concentration opened enough to permit a reminder of Mossa, and I wondered, as the evening passed and I paused to set more tea and order oatcakes for sustenance, whether she would return to my rooms or perhaps, if she had exhausted all the options of investigation in Valdegeld, travel straight back to Sembla to sleep. Surely she would return, or at least send a message—? But as the night continued I began to doubt, looking up from my work more and more often. The temperature had dropped, and I caught the sound of hail on the window, gritty fragments of Giant's constituent gases that had snagged and frozen in the atmoshield before pelting down on us.

At dawn I moved to my window seat. I had in my hand an overlay intended for sketching landscape plans, but it sank forgotten onto a cushion as I stared into the darkness. The narrow streets and high buildings in Valdegeld blocked any view of sunrise, but I watched the gas lamps wink off, watched shapes emerge from dimness, and so saw Mossa's figure as she turned down my street. Even from above she looked tired, but I indulged myself in watching her unseen for a moment longer before I went to order supper and draw a bath.

Mossa entered chilled and visibly weary.

"Did you find the student?" I asked, when she had unwrapped her cold outer garments and I had wrapped her in my arms.

"No," she said hoarsely. "But I found a pattern."

I unbundled her into the bath, banking my desire, and my curiosity, in deference to her comfort. Despite the addition of a second round of hot water, her fingers were still cool when the dumbwaiter dinged, and I brought a side table into the bathroom with the bowl of soup dumplings on it. She ate two, carefully sipping out the steaming broth before chewing. While we more temperately shared the rest she began to speak.

"Before I tell you about the case, I need to ask your permission. I want to know if you're willing to help me."

"Help you?" I leaned one hand into the bath, stirring the warm water gently with my fingertips. Perhaps I was too sleepy to understand. Last time, yes, I had made some connections that helped Mossa to resolve her investigation, but that had been a problem intimately interwoven with my research. Even if this missing person was a student at the university, that did not imply that I would have special knowledge.

"Yes, I think so. It is . . . unusual, yes. But not unheard of. I have the discretion to bring in someone to assist, in a cognitive capacity." Mossa moved uneasily in the water. "Investigators who . . . who do not pair well with other Investigators, let's say, sometimes do so, in order to have . . . another perspective, one not tethered to the same Investigator training, not subject to the same pressures and incentives." Fascinating. I was thinking about what such a policy might look like in the university context when she went on. "And when Investigators do attach someone, it is not uncommon for it to be . . . someone with whom they have an existing relationship of affection, since those are conversations that are likely to happen in that context."

I stared into the bath—away from Mossa herself—to

hide my smile, and my surprise. *An existing relationship of affection,* was it? "I'm happy to help if I can."

She was still eyeing me. "I know I do not have to worry about your discretion, Pleiti—" Many people, saying such a thing, would mean the opposite, but with Mossa I knew I could interpret it exactly as spoken—"and there is no specific Investigator responsibility attached, but I want to make sure you do not agree lightly." She had dropped her gaze to the water. "Some . . . partners feel that this draws the Investigator's work too much beyond its boundaries, that their relationship becomes excessively focused on that."

I put my hand on her knee—the closest part of her outside the water—and she stopped and looked at me. "You said there's no responsibility attached. So if it doesn't work, I can stop, yes?" She nodded, but her expression remained weighty, and I paused to think. True, our previous collaboration still haunted me, but only the parts that had involved direct attacks on me (and on Mossa, but if that was going to happen I'd rather be there to defend her) and on my beliefs. The rest of it . . . well, some of it had been horrible, but there was a satisfaction in engaging with that horrible rather than looking away. And thinking through the problems had been interesting; I had told her at some point that it was a pleasure to help her, a change from my studies, and I had meant it. "I agree. Because I want to. And I will tell you if I want to stop."

She held my gaze a moment longer and then, with another sigh, Mossa settled herself deeper into the bath and began. "You must understand that a startling percentage of cases brought to the Investigators deal with missing persons. It might even be considered the raison d'être of the service, if you looked back at the historical case that led to its establishment, not long after Giant was settled." She paused there, though I was listening attentively, never having known of the prevalence of absence, and then went on more concretely. "So as I told you last night, I had no reason to imagine that this case held anything sinister, or at least any more sinister than the common run."

"And now?" I asked, hollow.

"It is still little more than imagination, which is why I would like your thoughts." Mossa hesitated, tracing a circle on the surface of the bathwater with her finger. "Also because I am concerned about the possibility of something very sinister indeed."

- - - - - - - -

Chapter 3

The missing student was in his third year of Modern economics. His tutor had referred the Investigators after young Strevan had missed two sessions, although Mossa's inquiries discovered that she had no intention of doing so until pressed by Strevan's cling-rail teammate.

"The tutor was fortunate that I attended Valdegeld," Mossa commented. She had exited the bath by that point. I had immediately wrapped her in my warmest robe, quilted in pale indigo with undyed lapels and belt, and we were reconvened in the front room. "Another investigator might have been shocked at how unconcerned she was, and even I, considering that he's a third-year, thought it a bit blasé."

"Moderns," I said dismissively, and then caught myself. This was an investigation, and even in a semi-official role, no matter how Mossa might try to soften it, I did have responsibilities. "That is to say . . . they do tend to have more students per tutor than we do, and from what I've heard a somewhat laxer attitude towards, err, the more formal trappings of scholarship." That had not come out very well. "Ah . . . had he missed many other meetings?"

"Occasionally," Mossa said, leaning forward to pour the tea. "Though never before two in a row." The tutor seemed to believe that calling in the Investigators was unwelcome but conclusive in terms of her responsibility to her student, and her responses to questions had been perfunctory and off-hand. She was inclined to think that Strevan had shuttled off on holiday or to see family or friends, perhaps temporarily or perhaps giving up his university career altogether; not unheard of, although she couldn't point to any such indication in this case. Strevan had not been particularly behind in his work, nor had he evinced any despair as regards to finances or romantic inclination, though the tutor emphasized that the student wouldn't necessarily have told her his worries.

"She all but shooed me out of the room," Mossa recalled. "I suspect that, once she was forced to act by the insistence of the other scholar, calling the Investigators necessitated a lesser combination of paper- and footwork than any of the other options."

"The other scholar being the cling-rail teammate?"

Mossa gave me an approving nod, more warming than the tea in my cup. "The captain, in fact, of the cling-rail team."

Cling-rail was the most vaunted sport at Valdegeld, the one that we played, every year, against rival teams from Zaohui, Stortellen, and the other (lesser) universities of Giant. It had often struck me as odd, or perhaps merely interesting since historically the pattern was not uncommon, that a game now sacrosanct in the most exalted halls of learning and accompanied by endless encrusted traditions had such menial origins. Cling-rail derived from the early days of the settlement, when the rings encircling the planet, set on geosynchronous spins through carefully managed feats of engineering, were the only thing keeping the human population on Giant alive. They still were, come to think of it, but at the beginning, when there was only one, then two rings, basically untested, it must have felt far more precarious. Railcars at the time were few and rudimentary, and all monitoring and maintenance of the rings, as well as any unscheduled movement from one platform to another, had to be done by people in life-support suits. For these purposes they wore magnetic boots and, later, used magnetic bicycles. Even now, my parents' farming platform had a pair or two of those magnetic boots somewhere in storage, for emergencies. They were hardly ever used, or remembered, given that the Rings Authority was by now well-equipped and pro-active and railcars frequent, but the availability of such footwear, and of rings, on every platform meant that everyone had the opportunity to practice at least the rudimentary skills of cling-rail.

My parents' platform did not, of course, have the

dedicated chamber required for formal cling-rail matches; then again, neither did Strevan's team. It was (Mossa explained), a recreational intramural team, a shifting group of students and scholars who borrowed the Modernist cling-rail chamber when it was not otherwise in use for their practices and occasional matches against similar collectives. Despite the informality, the captain, a scholar named Redanen, asserted that Strevan's absence was indeed a cause for concern.

"He had missed five practices and two matches, and Redanen assured me that he would never, particularly the matches, without at least a message. He had been looking forward to one of the matches especially, the earlier one, for weeks—some rivalry with someone in his tutorial group."

"Could that have been a motive?"

"Redanen doubted it, said that not only are the matches not that serious, but Strevan isn't that good."

Indeed, Redanen had been unable to provide any reason for Strevan's disappearance or clues as to where he might have gone, voluntarily or involuntarily; there was, apparently, little socializing among the team.

Mossa had therefore spent most of the previous diurnal tracking down the friends and colleagues of the missing student and talking to his neighbors and the porters in his boarding house. What they had said matched with the tutor's account: nothing particularly remarkable about the student nor about his absence; it seemed equally possible that he had wandered off for an excursion and been delayed or that he had taken a drunken dare to walk a ring—with or without magnetic boots—between platforms and fallen forever. None of them shared the urgency of Redanen. Mossa had, on balance, little reason to dread anything other than having to file an incomplete case, and that, though always unsatisfying, occurred often enough to bear little sting.

Mossa paused here. We had already turned down the lights, and she watched the fire while I watched her face, the asymmetry caused by traumatic injury during our last case uncertain in the flickering light. I briefly cherished hopes that the story was over inconclusively, or, less probably, that we could continue it much later and in bed, but she at last put the mug she was cradling down on the table and continued.

"Today," she said, and then paused. "I must confess," she said, with more difficulty, paused again to lift the mug and sip, twitching a mueca at its undoubtedly cold contents. "When I said leaving a case incomplete is often done . . . I would have done it, for this one. I was entirely resigned to it, I was not shirking or rushing but—" Another sip, nearly a gulp. "Fog it all. I would have returned to Sembla, I would have considered my responsibility absolved, at least unless new information came to light independently. I only investigated today so as to have an excuse for staying with you last night."

Heat flashed over me swift as a sunrise, as a shock of recognition. I wanted to say something; in my idealized replays of that night I say, low but clear, *You don't need an excuse,* but I was too overtaken, and she went on before I had recovered.

"And I would have been wrong to go, because today I interrogated the records at the administrative offices. Pleiti, over this term and the last, *seventeen* people have gone missing from Valdegeld!"

Chapter 4

"Seventeen!" That was shocking enough to distract me even from the revelation of her affection. "But—how? How has this not been noticed?"

Mossa shook her head. "They were scattered: different faculties, halls, lodgings, ages, cohorts. Even when they were in the same department, they had different sub-specialties, different tutors. There are Investigator reports for only five of them, and from three different bureaux—it seems that my organization, like the university, needs to improve its data sharing. I found the rest by searching for unexcused absences or incomplete courses without any explanation, so it is possible that I included a few more innocent departures, but . . ."

"Seventeen," I agreed, glum. Even half that number was too many to ignore.

"I checked the numbers for previous years," Mossa added. "Seventeen does not just *seem* large, it is certainly an aberration. The term before last the number was eight; the term before that five; in the ten terms before that, it was never higher than three."

"I still don't understand why this isn't a major crisis. Or," a sour suspicion fostered by our experience during the last crisis, "is the university hiding it?"

"I don't believe so." Mossa sounded more thoughtful than certain. "The files had not been accessed recently. Most probably they have not shared the information across faculties or even departments."

"But . . . their families? Shouldn't they be doing something?"

"You must remember that none of them would know there are others missing; whether they are seeking on their own or reclaiming from the university, they are probably using the wrong scope. Also, you are thinking of students. Most of them were not." Mossa leaned forward, frowning now. "Five of the missing are scholars—there, I'm inclined to believe at least a few might have simply gone on vacation without giving notice. And seven are porters, kitchen workers, or other such support staff."

"Porters?" That seemed even more surprising, somehow, and I wondered with a chill whether I did not see porters as people enough to be kidnapped.

"Porters indeed. As with the scholars, they may simply have retired or quit without filing the proper laminates, but the sheer numbers suggest something more than chance at work. But . . . you **are** right, one would expect more outrage or concern from families. I wonder . . ." She broke off with a geste of frustration. "I need to know more about these people." Mossa's approach was based in an understanding of the characters and relationships of the actors in any particular case, and the narratives such configurations were likely to gravitate towards; learning about the personalities and connections of seventeen apparently unconnected people was going to be frustratingly time-consuming.

"Radiation." I wavered, unsure whether there was more, still longing for bed or at least further exploration of that interesting confession, but aware we were now on a ring very far-flung from the track of desire. I sat up from my cushion to pour more of the steeped tea for myself, more for something to do than because I thought it would provide me any real comfort. It did at least give me time to remember that she had asked for my help, not just as a listener or emotional support, but directly with her work.

"Were you able to learn anything else?"

She raised reddened eyes. "Very little. I spent the evening in the administrative offices, searching for connections among the missing." I shivered in sympathy; the records room was notoriously poorly heated. That explained the state in which she had returned. I seated myself beside her, and reached out to rub her arm; she leaned into me in return. "The few enlaces I could tie to even as many as fourteen of them were so common as to apply to vastly more students as well. But I am too tired now to think well; there could be a pattern I'm not seeing or a category I didn't think to investigate . . ." She leaned more, and I ran my hand over her hair.

"And that's where I can help, perhaps?" This was something anyone associated with Valdegeld could do, true, but she had come to me.

She had closed her eyes. "Your knowledge of the university may suggest something I wouldn't happen upon, yes . . . but it's not just that, Pleiti, I would appreciate your views on all of it, on anything. I want your brain, I want your insight . . ."

I saw the chance to switch rings and took it, turning my face to her. I did not rush, kissing her temple, her imperfectly healed cheek, the corner of her mouth, until she met my lips with hers.

Chapter 5

Mossa again woke and exited the bed before I did. Pushing myself unwillingly from the duvet after, I imagined the unknown like a coiled spring within her, driving her into motion.

I, on the other hand, required two refills of shibui tea and the warmth of a third, freshly brewed cup before I could formulate the question. "What is the plan for today?" I was formulating carefully in order to avoid pronouns; I wasn't sure if she expected to work alone or preferred me to accompany her, or even which option I was in favor of myself.

"I shall try to expand our"—*our!*—"knowledge base on the unreported missing. I hope to discover that the records are out of date and at least some are accounted for, which may make the pattern more clear; and in any case further information may reveal some explanatory commonality." She glanced up at me, steam from the tea veiling the corner of her face. "Do you not have work?"

"Not any that I can't— Ahh, stars, I do have a tutorial at eleven."

"Will you have time after that? I made a list of the few and partial links I could identify, you might see something I missed, or think of another category to check." She handed me the laminate, a piece of ancient Earth plastic salvaged and reshaped into a form convenient for carrying and scribing. There was a gas pen linked to it, for making notes, and the extruder machines in records had stamped Mossa's selections onto its leafs according to a coding that would, supposedly, facilitate pattern overlays.

"I can look," I said, doubtful that I would see something she hadn't. "Very well, then." We had had some practice saying *good-bye,* during these past months that we'd been shuttling back and forth between my home in Valdegeld and hers in Sembla, but we still didn't seem to have gotten the trick of it. "Good courage!" I tried, as she left, waving; it sounded overly dramatic.

I should have been reading until my tutorial, but instead I curled in my window seat to watch Mossa disappear at the corner. I looked over her list, still not rating my chances for an epiphany where Mossa's staggering intellect had failed to find insight. But then, she had not possessed the data set for very long, and had been exhausted or asleep for most of that time. *And* her knowledge of the university was neither as deep nor as current as mine. Somewhat encouraged, I read through the entries.

It was as she had said: a smattering of individuals so broad and diverse as to appear random. It was almost, I thought, arranging and rearranging the data with different filters and ordering, like a sample intended for statistical modeling, according to the Classical methodology. Perhaps that was the intent? I could not see how such an effort might combine usefully with disappearances, but I jotted down the idea in case Mossa could make something of it. It was only then that I glanced at the time. Swearing, I threw on the first clothes that came to hand, yanked my usual atmoscarf from its hook, and plummeted down the stairs and out into the chilly morning.

My tutee was a sweet young man named Tsvevo, Brecher Tsvevo, who brushed away my apologies for arriving late. He studied the ecosystem of New Zealand, with the usual challenge: we had the most thorough knowledge of species types and numbers from the twentieth and twenty-first centuries, but by then the collapse had already begun. Like most Classics scholars, Tsvevo believed that we needed to aim for a pre-industrial balance in hopes of longer stability, particularly given that any human resettlement would be fragile, the environment still recovering. His research, like mine, built on the theory that we would be better off modeling on relatively small (but self-sufficient) islands rather than trying to approximate the complexity of the full global ecosystem.

My role was to guide him through the process of

conducting research with optimal rigor: exhausting the resources of the university in search of corroboration or contradiction; plotting the data legibly and searchably; cross-referencing with studies at other locations. Eventually I would be attempting to lace together his findings with those of other researchers.

As every time since that conversation with Mossa about alternative methods of scholarship, I wondered if it was enough. I had recently spoken to a colleague in the Speculative department about doing a seminar for my tutees on how to evaluate and mark degrees of speculation in gap-filling hypotheses; I was thinking we might push that further. Perhaps a system analysis, with colored blocks representing relative roles and characteristics to remove the emotional connotations of specific animals, with comparisons and, and . . . some kind of shape to describe different ecosystem equilibriums in the examples we had . . . if only we could be more sure we were describing complete equilibriums, rather than incomplete and poorly understood maps based on data that was partial in both senses . . .

I came back to the moment. Tsvevo was politely pretending to be fascinated by his data, and we had not quite finished our usual time, but I sent him home, feeling a ghostly reverse of Mossa's guilt from the night before: I was shorting on my responsibilities to be with Mossa, or at least to savor the closeness of working on the same problem.

After Tsvevo had waved himself gratefully away (he did not seem to mind that we weren't putting in the full duration), I retreated into my office and looked again at the list. The collection of names and attributes still seemed entirely scattered on any plot I could imagine.

Unable to make sense of the grouping, I decided instead to concentrate on individuals. I didn't know anyone on the list, but surely I must know *of* some of them? The porters, whom I had scanned earlier with guilty fascination, were none of them from halls I was very familiar with; I might have passed some of them once or twice but I had no reason to remember them. I lingered over the entry for Mippala Noo, age thirty-eight, who had worked in the kitchens at Ha-Fien; I had eaten there often enough, as I had several friends in that hall and moreover it was not very far from my office. Perhaps I had passed Noo in the streets outside or in the corridors of the hall, but the image of his face called no answering echoes from my memory.

I rose and went down the corridor to the rudimentary kitchen for our cluster of bureaux to collect hot water for my teapot, reflecting as I walked, and absently nodded to my colleagues, and stood waiting beside the gas-ringed kettle, on the narrowness of the social confines in Valdegeld. I had read—somewhere, years ago—the hot-take paper of a societal psychologist at the time of settlement who worried that living on platforms would isolate humans into what he called "fragmentary subcultures," socially etiolated and fostering any number of dire mental and physical consequences. (As I recalled, that reading had been paired with another, contemporary piece arguing that after the years of crowding and close cohabitation on spaceships and stations, it would be wonderful for individuals and humanity as a whole to achieve relative isolation on relatively open platforms.) Valdegeld was large and populated and culturally rich beyond the imagination of that long-ago scholar, and we had managed to fragment our society nonetheless.

I settled into my office cushions while the tea steeped, continuing down the list. The scholar descriptions struck nearly the same chime of incongruity with me as the other workers: it seemed odd for so many adults, fully jobbed and seemingly self-reliant, to go missing.

All of the scholars but one were in the Speculative faculty, with the last in Modern, and while I didn't know any of them personally, surely I must be able to find some link. The Speculative scholars were in different departments: two in Futures, one in Syntheses, and one in Sciences. (The Modern one was a geographer, but after a mixed experience with that particular breed the last time I helped Mossa, I decided to leave that thread aside for the moment.) Whom did I know in Speculative who might be able to tell me more about these scholars?

I had not, before, had much interest in the Speculative area. It was not as banal as Modern (I had believed), but without the intense, long-cultivated rigor of Classical studies. (It is possible my perceptions were colored by the acquaintance of, in fact, one of Mossa's friends during our student days, a Speculative engineer somewhat scattered in personal habits and with brilliant but, I thought, unfounded imaginaries. Ta was, however, now one of the more celebrated in that field, and had even managed to collaborate with a Modern engineer on a space telescope that demonstrably functioned, so it was well past time for me to re-evaluate.) Still, we all knew that Classics would eventually need to work with the Speculative thinkers to achieve our aim of returning to Earth. There was, after all, no Classical basis for returning humanity en masse from another planet. But that often seemed hazily far-future; it was only with my recent interest in new approaches that I had become curious about how we might collaborate beyond that somewhat unexamined assumption.

I poured the tea into my cup, inhaling the steam and aroma, and followed the rings of my mind as I waited for it to cool, remembering events in the Speculative faculty, social gatherings that crossed disciplines, scholars I'd sought out to question.

Vecho Zei! Who better? I inhaled one scalding sip, then left the rest of my tea to stew as I took my satchel and hurried out the door.

Chapter 6

A brisk gale curled around the steeples of the Classical faculty, the fringes of a tempest that was passing to the south of us, and the sky was a clear and sulfurous yellow, a not infelicitous backdrop for my sudden exhilaration. I dodged quickly through the maze of alleys behind Uiven library in the direction of the Speculative campus, feeling agile and expert in the backways of Valdegeld, as I had once aspired to be when I arrived as a student from a remote farming platform.

Vecho Zei was the erai dueña of the Speculative faculty. An emeritus scholar well past the age of jubilation, she no longer gave tutorials or even lectures, but she knew everyone, remembered everything, and had even the stature to be allotted a tiny kantor in one of the Speculative halls where she read, napped, took tea with petitioners, advised her favored scholars and students, and occasionally stitched a few new sentences into the *The Blazing Giant,* her magnum speculation of Giant's settlement, inspired—and this was how I had met her, in fact—by a Classical work.

Indeed, the Classical and Speculative departments were tightly welded, like two rings joined by a platform. Classics, with the wealth of learning bequeathed from centuries of human knowledge-gathering on Earth and the noble mission of someday returning us to that planet, was unquestionably the heart of Valdegeld. But the Speculative field merited much of the approbation for our successful transfer to an unlikely planet, given the flights of imagination that engineered the chain of inhabitable space stations and the concept of rings and platforms to make a gas giant livable. If the Classics department found the formula for an eco-viable Earth, it would be the Speculative department that found ways to implement it.

The Speculative halls, libraries, and laboratories clustered around a central plaza—rather unusual for Valdegeld—that was adorned with examples of Speculative art. On that occasion I wandered among the statues and over the mosaics without registering them, my confidence in this initiative fading as I approached my destination. Zei might not be in her carrel; I had heard she appeared less and less, and now I remembered a chisme about her falling ill with fog-lung and associated pneumonia at the end of last term. Perhaps I could find someone else in the department who could tell me about the missing students and scholars.

As I approached along the spiraling corridor, however,

I heard voices coming from Zei's carrel. Encouraged that she was there, I hastened my steps, only to halt rather abruptly when I heard a reference to the recently deceased rector of Valdegeld.

"—was one of the most important officials at this university, we can hardly ignore it."

I couldn't have stated that it wasn't Zei who spoke, until I heard her voice, unmistakable with its aged creak and firm confidence and faint accent of Pyl, in response. "Can't you? I can assure you he would have been perfectly happy to ignore your *fallecimiento* if it served his purposes."

There was a pause in which I imagined the interlocutor managing their impulses. "I speak not personally, of course," the first voice said, with audible tonal control, "but for the university. In addition," with a slight elevation of volume to cover Zei's scoff, "there will be those people, however unlikely it seems, who feel bereaved. It is only appropriate to offer them an opportunity . . ."

I puffed out breath involuntarily. They were justifying a remembrance service for Rector Spandal! Truly (to quote a Classical text), *Evil men are ceded importance even after they die, when it no longer matters to them, and only affects us.*

"So you want to please everyone, as usual," Zei was saying sardonically when I was able to align my brain on their voices again. "And you expect me to do the orbital mechanics for you?"

It occurred to me that I had no reason to listen illicitly to this, and that, in fact, I had no desire to hear the rest of it, licitly or not. I rapped quickly on the door and stepped in.

They looked startled to see me (in Zei's case, less startled than grumpy; or perhaps that was left over from the previous conversation and she didn't care about my appearance in the least); but I was at least as smacked. It had not occurred to me that Zei's interlocutor might be Ananakuchil Mars, dean of the Classics faculty, and my jefe.

Ta recovered first. "Pleiti," ta said, nodding. "Publish much lately?"

It was a standard, ritualized greeting among scholars; the verb "to publish" was antiquated and only tenuously related, etymologically or practically, to how we distributed our work. I wasn't sure whether it was my recently increased association with Mossa, who always looked at social conventions sideways, or a tension in Mars's intonation that made the meaningless words sting. I skipped the usual responses (*Waiting on reviews* or *Ever more citations,* depending on one's mood), only returning the nod.

Mars did not seem troubled by this, but ta did feel it necessary to impose on me, stiffly, the plans for the rector's memorial. "Since the body has been found," ta said, and I wondered if the blame I felt came from ta or from myself.

It was not a pleasant conversation, and I considered myself lucky, all in all, to escape after only a dozen or so fraught exchanges. Any thoughts I might have had of remaining to speak privately with Zei were obviously in vain; the elder waved us both away with the stump of her left arm, eyelids sagging. I did turn into the factotum's office, mostly as an excuse for not walking out with Mars, but the primary was out and I lacked the vim, at that point, to wait or compose a message. I trudged home and climbed to my rooms, where I found Mossa vibrating around the salon in a coil of nervous energy.

Chapter 7

"Pleiti!" She whirled on me as soon as I came in the door. "You've returned, and not before time. We have much to—"

I had shed my atmoscarf and turned back to her. "Mossa." I did not mean it to sound so blank, and by contrast to my usual delight in seeing her it must have seemed even flatter. I noted that the fire was banked low, as though Mossa didn't require its warmth or brightness.

"Pleiti," Mossa repeated, but in quite a different tone. She was examining me with quiet intensity. "Are you well?"

I spilled cleanser on my hands, then jabbed at the fire button, urging forth heat. "They're holding a ceremony of remembrance for Rector Spandal." I turned to her again at last, my anger bubbling up through my shock. "Can you fathom it?"

Mossa had gone to the intercom, presumably to order tea; she stood stilled, and when she replied it was in the controlled tone that expressed as much anger as my useless attack on the fire dimmer. "I suppose, from their perspective, it is a refusal to admit that they chose wrong in their officialdom."

"Well, they did!" I threw myself down on the cushions. "How dare they?"

She settled more deliberately beside me. "You seem unusually incensed. Was there something more?"

I rubbed my palms over my face. They smelled, not unpleasantly, of the disinfectant. The pause grew long, but my tears at least had retreated and I spoke without tremors. "I ran into Dean Mars. Ta asked me to speak at the memorial."

Mossa's eyebrows shot up. "That seems foolish." The dumbwaiter dinged, and she rose and went for the tray.

"I refused," I said, somewhat anticlimactically, wondering whether she had already deduced that result from my character, from the narrative she was constructing of these events. I wasn't sure I would have predicted it myself. I was not accustomed to refusing the university.

"I can only applaud that decision," Mossa said mildly, busying herself with the tea.

But the dean had asked me; had thought it was a good idea; had clearly expected me to say yes. I kept my eyes on the flames, said the first thing that came to mind. "People keep expecting me to be upset about the rector, but I think so much more about Rechaure." A fanatic who had ranted about the end of the world on a street corner, the victim of Rector Spandal's far more toxic fanaticism.

"That seems reasonable to me," Mossa said. "Leaving aside that Spandal nearly killed us—"

"They do get that, they don't expect me to mourn him, necessarily," I felt obliged to explain. "But they do think the whole experience will have been more weighty, more traumatic . . . Dean Mars said ta thought speaking at the memorial would be *therapeutic* for me . . ." Mossa snorted. ". . . and I keep thinking about Rechaure instead."

"As I said. Leaving aside his ill will, Spandal chose his risks and suffered only the consequences." She didn't have to say that the end-of-the-world preacher, by contrast, had been killed; and only because of a chance encounter, because of the most attenuated chance that he might reveal a fraction of a secret by mentioning it.

"Also because I knew the rector better."

"Did you?" Mossa said this not with disbelief, but with a faint distaste, as though she thought I was unfortunate to have been put in such a position. But when I thought about it, had I really known the rector any better? I had probably heard them each say roughly the same number of words—perhaps even more from Rechaure, if you counted all the repeats of his rantings. And if Rechaure's had been rantings, the rector's had been rote. Not only mostly lies, but statements that I had not considered of any substance even before I had reason to question their truth.

The people who gave him more importance, who

thought that I should, didn't really mean that I had known him better; only that I could relate to him more; that we were, because of status or affiliation, somehow more alike.

Too disgusted and ireful to sit still, I pushed to my feet and took to pacing in an attempt to shake away the brume of my musings. "It's far less worthy of our time than the problem of the missing Valdeans. I could speculate from your status when I arrived that you've learned something?"

Mossa brightened, took an incautious sip of her tea, hissed in air. "Indeed," she managed, in between puffs over the surface of her cup. "Indeed. I have learned of another missing person—" I groaned in dismay, and she held up a triumphant gesture. "—and, a clue!"

"A clue?"

"Well, at a minimum a thread," Mossa said, not sounding perturbed at all.

She had received permission from the Modern faculty to search Strevan's rooms. There, she had found some messages indicating a relationship—"What *sort* of relationship exactly was not clear"—with another student, named Zebaia Elemaya. "They corresponded, not so constantly as to be considered namourades or close friends *necessarily*, but certainly enough to suggest she was worth talking to." But when Mossa went to her rooms, the porter hailed her without surprise, assuming someone else had referred the Investigators. "He hadn't seen her for days, had been concerned enough to start thinking of coming to us himself."

"That . . . does not seem like a good thing?" I said

cautiously. Mossa had ordered desiccated tomatoes and warm polenta, and the nourishment was notably improving my perspective on the world, but even so.

"No," Mossa agreed. "But it is a break, because now we have found two missing people with a clear relationship."

"Perhaps they're not missing for the same reason as the others, who all seemed so unconnected?"

"Perhaps not. I am, for the moment, cautiously inclined to consider plot lines where they are linked. But in either case, this is the one I was asked to investigate, there is no reason not to follow it up."

There was still a suppressed excitement about her that even a trail to follow did not seem to explain. "Go on." She didn't answer, her lips curving, eyebrows rising in challenge. I swirled more piment spices into the polenta and scooped up another swallow, thinking what she wanted me to ask. "How did they know each other?"

"They grew up together."

"Oh? What remote platform are we traveling to now, then?" It had not escaped me that not only Mossa's but my bags were packed and sitting by the door.

Mossa's rare smile widened into a rarer, feral grin. "Io."

"And . . . you expect me to accompany you to the moon?"

The smile fell from her face. She put down her cup. "I—I don't expect—you don't have to join. But last time, when I almost left without you, you were so upset—"

"Mossa." I put my cup down as well, perhaps with more force than was necessary, but I was trying to keep my voice calm and the fury had to go somewhere. "I was angry last time because you *didn't give me a choice.* It's not about whether I go with you on every journey or do not, it's about you asking me what I want to do! And listening!"

"Oh, well then, that's all right then, isn't it?" She sounded relieved but still wary. "I am not forcing you to join, I . . . I suppose I didn't ask, as such, did I?"

"You packed my bags," I said, as dryly as I could in the face of her obvious ovinity.

"Well, but, that's just because we're rather short on time. I promise you, Pleiti, I will not be in the least offended if you don't wish to come, although I would vastly prefer if you did." The flare of warmth I felt at that, like a foolish fire springing to life in a hearth, evaporated the last of my anger. "But if you *do* want to, we should leave in, oh—" She glanced at the timepiece on the wall. "—fifteen minutes?"

I sighed, hurried a last few bites, and went to use the lavatory and wash my face before what would undoubtedly be a fraught experience.

Chapter 8

We took the railcar to Jaosou, one of the two shuttle ports with service to Io. It was a longish journey, with a change at Trubrant that included an irritating wait, during which Mossa disappeared into the shopping area of the station to return with her bag visibly bulging—gifts from the mainland, I concluded sourly, my insides writhing at the thought of the extraplanetary flight, at the time I would have to spend away from my research and my students and my rooms.

I had never considered Io an appealing destination (despite Mossa's connection; odd, really, because that should have at least piqued my interest), and my one visit had done little to change my inclination. There were excellent, immutable reasons why the settlement there had failed, and I didn't quite see the point in a long, difficult journey to the site of that failure as well as of other, even more deplorable incidents. We could learn about that history perfectly well from the comfort of our stable, non-lava-spewing platforms. However, I could not deny the—thin, but extant—investigatory justification for this visit or Mossa's greater expertise, and so I boarded the railcar when it arrived and kept my grumbles tacit. Our wagon was, unfortunately, crowded on both legs of the trip, so we did not discuss the case, although Mossa did share some fried breadfruit on that second tranche; apparently not all her purchases in Trubrant had been for Ionians.

The shuttles to Io ran regularly but, due to the scant traffic, infrequently, which was why Mossa had hurried us out of the apartment. I was grateful she had left me time to eat first, and purchased snacks for the train: by the time we got to the shuttle port I was in no mood to commit food to my stomach. I had gone so far, as we approached Jaosou, to consider a stasis pill to get through the trip, but the thought of explaining such a weakness to Mossa, as well as the waste of the medicament, stopped me from acting on it.

"I won't be able to stay past the next return," I warned Mossa, studying the schedule during our brief wait for embarkation. I had little desire to be on Io any longer than necessary, but I also could not ignore my responsibilities at the university, especially as she had not given me opportunity to make alternate arrangements. "There are three days between that and the following one, and I would miss two tutorials, not to mention getting behind in my research."

"Ma'alesh." Mossa did not sound troubled. "I'll stay on longer alone if I have reason to. In any case I'll appreciate any insight you can give me during the time we have."

The stubby vehicle we boarded looked nothing like the rocket we had narrowly avoided being incinerated by in our previous escapade, especially when arranged horizontally for boarding; but then, it required far less propulsion—and, given that it had a trio of human pilots, far less circuitry as well. To distract myself through the ratcheting tilt to vertical and the solid shove spacewards, I thought of the many perilous vehicles of the classical era: ships balancing over uncharted ocean depths; the early, rickety airplanes and early, rickety spaceships—it was not helping.

Towards the front of the cabin, an attendant dressed in scholars' robes displayed a diagram showing how the course of the shuttle avoided the plasma torus, then explained the radiation shielding, concerns that I found somewhat abstract. The shuttle bounced on some inconsistency in the atmosphere and I gripped the seat handle.

"Have you been on a shuttle before?" Mossa, as usual, had not missed the minute gesture.

"Once." On an exhale I mouthed the lema of a prayer, a ritual to relax my jaw muscles, then inhaled and continued. "In university, there was a trip . . ." I stopped, remembering that she knew quite well about that trip and the circumstances under which she had not joined. Mossa evidently recalled as well; she had turned to look out the window, though there was as yet nothing to see but fog. "It's just, not being on a rail. It feels so unpredictable, like we could spin off in any direction . . ."

"It's not uncontrolled," Mossa said, not condescendingly but cautiously, as though she wasn't certain what to say to assuage my worries. "Indeed, it would be vanishingly unlikely for the pilots to make that sort of error. Or, I suppose, choice."

She continued in that vein. It also was not helpful. I wished she would put her arm around me, or something, *something* to be comforting. But she wouldn't, she wasn't going to. Not unless I told her to, and that negated too much of the benefit to be worthwhile.

"Do you go back often?" I asked, mostly to shift the conversation.

"To Io? Not very often, although I have been a few times for work over the past several years. It's not an easy trip to make on personal resources, I'm always glad of the excuse to go."

Odd, I had not thought of this as a benefit for her, an excursion she would *want* to make; a homecoming, even. I wondered whether that exposed my prejudices about Mossa or about Io. I wondered whether that emotion was why she had been so eager to bring me along. "Your family?" We passed out of the last tendrils of planetary gas, and in the window beyond Mossa the stars gleamed, static and far sharper than my usual view of them. It helped, a little.

"My father died some years ago—" ("May his memory be a blessing," I murmured, and she dipped her chin in acknowledgment) "And my mother emigrated to Giant." Helped, no doubt, by Mossa's career.

"Do you have connections on Io still then? With

your . . ." I knew that as her parents had both been migrant workers, she had been brought up partly in a crèche, as was a fairly frequent custom on Io, but I found it difficult to say the word. *Was* it the sort of place one visited after one left?

But a small smile tilted Mossa's lips. "Indeed, friends and honorary aunties and so on. I will make the rounds."

I pretended to settle myself back in my seat, as though I were relaxing, though in fact I was using the movement to distract myself through another few moments of this precipitous, ridiculous flight. I kept my head tilted to the left, so that I could keep my gaze on those brilliant stars, reassuringly stable, and Mossa's quarter-profile. The conjunction was almost enough to reconcile me to this uncomfortable journey.

Chapter 9

There is a romantic notion about standing on planetary material, as though your body somehow knows whether the solidity beneath your feet continues to a core or is simply a metallic crust suspended on gas. Or perhaps the relevant quality is whether it is natural or constructed? In any case, I felt nothing of the sort. I was, naturally, relieved to disembark from the shuttle—no one could mistake *that* for solid ground!—but I felt no equivalent to the Classical concept of "sea legs," whereby one would become accustomed to the sway of a ship and then stagger about when on (supposedly) unmoving land; nor did I feel any urge to kiss the sulfuric compounds of Io's surface. Instead I appreciated the dully varying colors, the menacing cones and the sunken plateaus in various stages of cultivation, with a decidedly jaded eye.

On our educational university visit to Io, the chaperoning scholar's lectures had lingered long on the evils of terraforming, with a regretful footnote admitting that we on Giant still benefited from the soil cycle that had been grafted into Io's plateaus. We had visited the memorial to the workers sacrificed in that effort (recognizing its bulky statuary from the back on our way to our inn on this visit, I could not help wondering how the planned remembrance for Rector Spandal would compare). Indeed, our student trip seemed to have been mainly memorials. I also recalled a horrifying dramatic presentation about the people forced to choose between facing Earth's apocalypse, or escaping at the behest and patronage of the corporation they worked for but leaving their families and friends behind.

When the richest had settled Io, no one had thought it would be possible to live on Giant. It wasn't their unwillingness to offer space in their meager early spacecraft that had bred the most enduring anger: it was that the first escapees from the apocalypse had been ready to use force to fend off those latecomers who had scraped together the means to travel there on their own.

The scoffed-at platforms had survived on Giant, though it was decades before they were any more pleasant to live on than a space station. In the meantime, the unstable geography of Io and, in no small part, the limited pool of settlers who had been permitted to land, had all but doomed that colony.

Some of the separated familial branches had been reunited generations later; others had been lost; still others kept the breach open in continuing feuds. More generally,

the fury at those wealthy exclusivists had left a lasting resentment against Ionians, even if many of them had been
essentially indentured workers. Combined with the more
limited opportunities available on Io for schooling and
cultural enhancement, immigrants to Giant faced a persistent if often unspoken stigma.

Those divided families, though . . . "Perhaps that's it,"
I exclaimed. Mossa and I were eating at the hotel, under
an arbor strung with leafy vines. I didn't feel quite safe
being out of doors, and that unease had combined with
the adrenaline-exhaustion from the flight, the slightly in-
toxicating mix of breathable gases manufactured by the
atmoshield, and the disorientation of being on a different rotation schedule to loosen any guards I had on my
tongue. "A generational dispute between families, threatened by the Ionian branches arriving in Valdegeld . . ."
There was even wine, supposedly produced from grapes
grown on the very plants tangling over our heads, although I was not entirely convinced.

Mossa, lounging on a slatted chair, looked entirely
at ease. "I hadn't realized you watch novelas, Pleiti," she
commented.

I was too flown to even be dismayed, although not too
much so not to jump at the sound of a volcano erupting
in the distance.

"Any word," Mossa went on, apparently not noticing the
faint boom, "the other missing people were not from Io."

"But it could still be the explanation for these two," I
insisted. "Strevan and this . . . Elme—Elamn—"

"Elemaya." Mossa was visibly amused, which was

adorable and humiliating and also very unusual. Unable to parse it, I pushed on.

"We don't know that they're connected to the others! Or perhaps the others are from the branch of the family that settled Giant! It's been so many generations, they could easily have spread across platforms and seem entirely unrelated."

Mossa just laughed, and threw the last crumb of her hard winter-sorghum roll at me. It was extraordinary to see her in what, I realized, could be considered her native habitat. "They are not. Come, tell me: Do you think this is what wine tasted like on Earth?"

I examined my glass doubtfully. "Surely there's been research on this by some Classical gastronomist or other?"

"No. I looked."

"I'll try to set someone on it then, it could be worth a dissertation, or at least a paper . . ." I took another sip, swirled it in my mouth the way people did in Classical media. "Perhaps . . ." It wasn't repugnant, though the taste clung in my mouth in an odd way. "Classical accounts make much of the soil that the vines are cultivated in, so one assumes it would be somewhat different . . ." I gazed out at the alien landscape of Io: potted with peaks and rifts, intensely irrigated, blooming with Earth plants tweaked to accommodate the atmosphere and soil. "Then again, I suspect our palates are too untrained to catch such subtle differences."

"Close enough then," Mossa said, with that surprisingly easy smile. "Well. We've both been awake for quite a while, and the adjustment should be approached gently in any case. Shall we sleep before we start our search?"

Io, tidally locked with Giant, had a significantly longer diurnal cycle. I did not pretend to grok what that meant for either our sleep or investigation schedules (much less how people managed to live in such a place) but presumably Mossa had that all under control, and I was weary. I raised my glass in acquiescence and, after draining it, followed her inside.

The inn was only one story, and was constructed out of some sort of light, flexible material, presumably so that it wouldn't collapse on us if Io's seismic activity peaked, or possibly so that it wouldn't hurt very much if it did. The room the attendant led us to was dim and strangely comfortless; it took me a moment to recognize the absence of a hearth. There were also two beds, both of them exceedingly narrow. I wondered (as we washed, undressed, and folded ourselves separately into our separate bedclothes) whether the inn had made an assumption, or if Mossa had specified the arrangements when she booked the room, or perhaps if it was the only type of room they had.

It should have been easy to sleep, from the combination of exhaustion and the ebbing adrenaline of the flight. And while Mossa and I were not together as often as I would have liked, we had shared a bed the previous two nights: I should not be starved for her.

And yet. I lay in that tiny, rather uncomfortable bed, breathing the strangely organic and sulfuric smells of the air seeping through the poorly sealed window, and yearned. Her bed was separated from mine by an arm's length: if I stretched I might touch her half-bare shoulder.

If I woke her, would she reach back with welcome in her eyes, would we turn the constrictive size of the single bed to our advantage? Or would she turn her head to her pillow instead? Was she too exhausted, was she ashamed of me in her often maligned homeland, was she in the throes of emotions too complicated to overlay with our relationship? I sweated, despite the chill, and thought of the night before and the night before that, thought of her fingertips and her lips, melted into my sweat-damp sheets, stretched my arm time and again and always pulled back before I could touch her. Why did she not wake from the fierceness of my desire, from my heat? And why, why was I not satisfied?

- - - - - - - -

Chapter 10

The father of Strevan lived in a type of construction known as a hobbit house, presumably because no matter how vague your grasp of Classical literature, that still sounded cozier than *bunker*. It was built into an artificial slope in the plateau, and the door, I was disgusted to see, wasn't even round.

Strevan Senior—his given name was Mas—opened the door with a blank unsurprised look; Mossa had sent a message ahead, probably while I was still struggling to pry my eyes open. He led us along the dim interior with only the most minimal of greetings and courtesies, gestured vaguely at the stiff-woven seating in a low room, mumbled something about tea, and disappeared back into the corridor. I appreciated the effort; we had breakfasted (surprisingly well) at the inn, but after my difficult night I was ready to absorb all the caffeine I could get.

The room we were in had a rounded ceiling and no windows, although a scene of a vibrantly colored valley glowed, humming with effort, from a square frame on the wall. I looked on it with fondness—hideous, but my grandmother had used one; they had been popular on Giant when she was a child. Hers, I remembered, had been a reconstruction of the landscape her ancestors might have viewed (or supposedly so; it now occurred to me, very belatedly, to wonder whether the entire trend was a scam; who, after all, would be able to refute the image?) and I rose and sauntered over to examine it more closely. I couldn't identify the location, assuming that it was intended as somewhere specific, but listening to its unending buzz I did come up with a question.

"What do they use for fuel here?" I was rather pleased with myself for even thinking of this; on Giant, with a literal and enormous planet of gas at our disposal, it rarely occurred to us to consider energy as anything but ambient.

"Don't know much about Io, now, do you?" Mas Strevan had returned, the tray rattling in his hands as he edged through the door. "It's thermal, of course. The missus works at the thermal plant, running maintenance and such." He looked like a man who lived in a bunker, blinking too often as though perpetually expecting an explosion just overhead to test the structural integrity of his roof.

Then Mossa offered him noncommittal condolences, and I mentally flagellated myself for criticizing the stricken expression of a man whose child was missing.

"He hasn't been gone very long," Mossa was reassuring him. "And we have a very good record of finding people—in part due to our efforts to speak with their proximals, even when they're physically distant. Can you tell us if you knew about any concerns your son had recently, any issues . . ."

"Of course," Strevan's father said, fidgeting with his teacup. "Of course we were worried about him going to such a dangerous place, those platforms just hovering there over all that gas and cold, I can't comp how anyone could live there."

I felt a pressure on my leg, looked down, identified it as Mossa's hand, glanced up to meet her eyes, and closed my gaping jaw.

"And the university, that is, the town it's in, from what I've heard there's all sorts of things go on there—" Again I was ready to bristle in disbelief; Valdegeld was an exceedingly cultured platform, very well thought of as a place to live, and even if it was only natural that the students occasionally got up to mischief, that only added to its charm. ". . . And tall buildings, they say, that anyone could fall off of anyhow—"

"Quite so, quite so," Mossa said agreeably, "but we were wondering about any concerns *he* had? He seems to have adjusted to the university admirably . . ."

Mas Strevan took a noisy sip, put his cup down. "Well

now, well now. I'm glad to hear of that. We were worried, as I said, but, Shaonam"—his son's given name—"explained to us how ... how ... how he could learn engineering, you know, to build things. Help our situation here."

Mossa's face was immobile, which read as a frown to me.

"And," she pressed gently, "any recent stresses, or even changes that he might have mentioned?"

Strevan Senior turned his cup half a circle, then back again. "Not recent, as such," he mumbled. "Haven't had much news from him recent."

"When was the last time you heard from him?" Again, her voice was calm, but I was aware of the urgency beneath her stillness.

"Oh, hmm." He thought about it, turning the cup again. "Perhaps ... a month? Two months?"

"Ours?" Mossa asked.

His eyes flicked up to hers. "Yes," he replied after a pause. "Ours."

I would have waited patiently, asked her when we were alone or investigated on my own, but Mossa murmured, "At least three months on Giant" from the corner of her mouth, and I felt the heat of embarrassment flooding my face.

"Did he have a friend named Elemaya?" I asked, brazenly out of turn.

Mas Strevan frowned. "What, them? Of course we know of them. Never had any cause to mix with them."

"He didn't know Zebaia Elemaya?" Mossa asked.

"I don't know that one, in particular. But they're from

over in Chaac. And anyway, they're descended from originals, so."

Even with weighted clothes, I was finding walking in Io's lighter gravity a rather perplexing challenge, and so we were some ways from Strevan's very un-hobbit-like hole before I noticed Mossa's air of restrained jubilation.

"I told you the journey would be worth it," she said at last, either having decided we were far enough to speak privately or realizing that I finally had attention to spare.

I grumbled something to indicate I was listening without committing myself to anything but crankiness. Probably I needn't have made the effort, as Mossa went on almost without a pause: "There was nothing, absolutely nothing up till now, to indicate that Strevan thought of returning here after graduation."

"He might not have decided yet," I inserted, feeling that I might as well put my mood to good use and act the contrarian.

"True, but everything I learned about his character on Giant suggested rather an inclination to status *there*, to showing them what he could do, proving himself and reaping the rewards. The discrepancy suggests deception, ambition, and such similar weaknesses that might be exploited by someone wishing to do him harm." She glided on, thoughtful.

"We still don't know that anyone did him harm," I pointed out from her wake.

"They could equally provide motivation for him to disappear on his own, although I do not yet have a scenario for that." During the pause that followed, the ground rippled beneath our feet: I froze, or tried to, but Mossa barely seemed to notice, adjusting her footing and returning to her theme: "Moreover, it seems clear that he and Elemaya met on Giant, rather than knowing each other here."

"Another mistaken assumption on the part of ignorant Gianters."

I expected Mossa to cock an eye at me, instantly deduce that I felt out of balance—literally as well as figuratively, since I was struggling to keep a steady pace instead of alternately bounding and bobbling—and respond by ostentatiously pretending to ignore the gambit. Instead, she apparently did ignore it. "And she's from an original family, as well."

"What does that mean?" I hadn't wanted to ask, but I didn't know when I'd have a chance to research, and besides it sounded like one of those local idioms impossible to look up.

"That the family traces itself to the original settlers of Io." She noted my incomprehension. "The CEOs."

"What?" I sputtered, shocked out of my sulk. "You mean . . ." I gestured vaguely in the direction of the monuments and memorials we could see looming from the entrance to the town. "Those terrible people? I'm not sure if I'm more shocked that their families can still be identified so many generations later or that they actually admit to it."

Mossa made a mueca of distaste. "It is, indeed, odd.

Some people, I suppose, will claim anything that distinguishes them from the majority, no matter how disgraceful. I should say, they do not have the cachet in Ionian society that they would like. I could name one or two, but only because I have come in contact with them personally. It's not," she glanced down as the surface bulged slightly beneath us, "something we talk about much."

It occurred to me that she was, quite possibly, ashamed, or at the very least somewhat embarrassed. And indeed, the idea of the descendants of those comemierdas still believing themselves special and apart played into stereotypes of Ionians that had, doubtless, often been held against Mossa.

"Will we be visiting them, then?" I asked, in a clumsy attempt to change the topic.

Mossa scowled at the horizon. "*I* certainly will. And, yes, I would like to have your reaction. But we must leave at once to get to Chaac and back in time for your return, and it will not leave us time for anything else." She caught my curious look (I had not been aware that there was anything else to do), and crinkled her nose ruefully. "I had thought to visit my old crèche with you, but we will have to forgo that."

At that moment, and against all expectations, I resolved that I would find a way to return to Io with Mossa, however unpleasant the journey. Perhaps at end-of-term holidays? Maybe I could even bring myself to look forward to it.

- - - - - - - -

Chapter 11

The seismic substructure of Io being what it was, rail-based transportation of any kind was out of the question, so for our journey I was once again without the comfort of rings; only this time, it was Mossa driving. She claimed to be exceedingly competent with the vehicle, a type of "buggy" according to the local nomenclature, that roved lightly across the inconstant ground powered by some sort of battery. The journey, traversing atmoshielded corridors laid out for this purpose, was in many ways arduous; but it was also striking and strange. We jounced past tangled stretches of agriculture, cultivated in the tradition of two centuries earlier, with symbiotic species growing inter-twined; in one field we saw farmworkers inserting the in-sects by hand, as my grandparents had done on Giant. We saw four eruptions and drove along an active lava flow, with Mossa constantly reassuring me as to the safety of our roadway.

Still, the sight that most astonished me was not of Io at all. Most of the inhabited areas of Io stand, of course, on the "dark" side of the moon, away from Giant; to face the enormous planet would mean forgoing almost all direct sunlight. However, Ionian settlements sprawled and stretched in odd ways to avoid the estimated range of volcanic eruptions and other documented seismic disturbances (the maps had always put me in mind of outreaching synapses), and from some areas the rounded edge of Giant peered over the horizon, bafflingly large. We traveled along one road (I later suspected that Mossa had chosen it on purpose; we arrived at the perfect time for the full effect, which I believe she must have orchestrated) that crested a ridge and wove out in a long loop suddenly providing us a view of almost all of Giant, bright and staggeringly beautiful with its writhing, colored gases.

The vision warmed me in some way—with pride or maybe aesthetic appreciation of my home—but it also unnerved me. Seeing Giant like that, at a distance, crystallized for me the unease I had been registering without articulating since we arrived: a fundamental uncertainty in the viability of where I was. It was the hidden suspicion that our buggy might, on one of its over-eager bounces, completely lose the trick of gravity and float away into the firmament; or that the explosive terrain beneath us, despite its persistence for millennia, might collapse. It was a mistrustfulness, a sense of being unsafe, an edgy awareness that unexpected disruption could occur at any moment. I wanted to go home, where I felt safe.

It occurred to me, as we continued our journey in silence, that when the first refugees from Earth had arrived on Giant—and, for that matter, on Io—they must have felt much the same.

We arrived at last at a fairly prepossessing gate in an imposing wall, a sight which made me feel as though I had walked, or bounced rather, into a Classical novel: there are few private grounds on Giant, and anyone affluent enough to have such space and feel the need to protect it is likely to have their own platform. There was even (to my secret delight) a gatehouse, and when Mossa, who seemed to know the way of things, slid her fingers over the button announcing us, a rather gumptious mid-elderly man sortied out to greet us.

"Here for the tour?" he asked, without much encouragement.

"Not a bit," Mossa replied quellingly. "We'd like to speak to someone about Zebaia Elemaya. This is her home, yes?"

"Was until she decided to go to university planetside." He sniffed. "Well, I'm her uncle." I had been hoping for *elderly retainer.* "Her brothers are around somewhere as well, and one of her sisters. You might as well come in, I suppose."

The gatehouse was somewhat larger than it had appeared, and to my surprise the man led us into a salon there, pausing, without offering us seats, to ask who we were.

"I'm from the Investigators' office on Giant. And this is my copine and colleague."

The man sniffed again, eyeing us sidelong. "I just hope you two are doing your part for repopulation otherwise."

I barely had time to register the conflicting scour of embarrassed anger and an urge to laugh before Mossa launched into a discourse. "Population has long been used as an empty alarm to encourage or discourage various, usually individual, behavioral choices. This is apparent from the frequent points in history when both population growth and low birth rates were framed as threats, often reflecting an underlying opinion as to which segments of population the speaker desired to perpetu—"

He interrupted, but by that point, I would have too. "You can hardly compare," he said hotly, "the underhanded racism of those days with concern about the survival of our species now!"

"I can and am," Mossa said. "We have human settlements scattered across a planet and three moons; on the basis of having multiple semi-stable habitats, at least, we are somewhat less precarious than the species has been at any point in history, when an adverse event affecting Earth would have destroyed us all. And I see no reason why our goal should be *as large a population as possible* or even *a population similar to that in Earth's later stages*. As you yourself suggest, there's little reason to hold those later ages up as a model for anything, and, more to the point, the limitations on food production suggest we let our population grow gradually if grow it must."

"I really don't see—"

"No," Mossa agreed, "I don't think you do. We'd rather speak to one of Zebaia's siblings. We'll wait here," she added, when he didn't immediately give up on his gaping.

Fortunately for them as well as for us, and perhaps most of all for the investigation, Zebaia's brothers (her sister was busy in the garden, and we did not insist) were cast from a far different mold.

"Oh stars," the oldest brother, Laruch, groaned. "I'm sorry. We really shouldn't let Uncle Whist anywhere near the public. Only, he's awfully good at the tour."

They had pointed out the object of the tour on our way through the grounds: thick slabs of concrete tilting out of the ground, and glimpsed within them, like sepals of a flower or the craggy glimmering heart of a quartz, a confusion: tangled wires and shattered silicon, mildewed cushions, something with bright printed letters on it. "Authentic," the younger boy said proudly, but Laruch squelched him with a glance. "A mix of authentic and . . . authentic reconstructions," he corrected, "although even those are quite old."

They had brought us to a building they called *the cottage,* where they offered us yogurt tea, and biscuits with an interesting waffle print on them that did not make up for the lack of taste. "Sorry, honeycomb was skint this year," Laruch explained, refilling our mugs.

It was all odd—the yogurt tea, never my favorite, had

a strange tang, as though perhaps the milk came from an unusual animal—but it still felt more realer, or more present, or easier in some way, than any other interaction I'd had on Io.

"I'm not sure you know," Mossa began carefully, "but your sister has been missing for a few days. It might be nothing," she hastened to add, as the brothers looked at each other with consternation. "It hasn't been very long and, lamentably, students often go off somewhere without telling the right people, worry everyone, and then reappear later."

"But you're *here*," Laruch said. "It must be serious for you to come all the way out here."

"There was another Ionian student missing," I said, aiming for soothing. "We were on the moon anyway, so we wanted to follow up."

"It doesn't matter," said the younger brother. "I hope nothing's happened to her, but whether she left or someone else made her leave, it means they won't let us go."

"They might! Our parents don't know about it yet, do they?"

"No," Mossa responded, watching them. "Not from us."

"Do you want to go to Valdegeld so much?" I asked, wondering about the uncle's evident disapproval when he had mentioned their sister going.

"Anywhere," Laruch said fervently, and his brother nodded enthusiastic agreement. "Say, that's an idea—maybe we could blame it on Valdegeld specifically, and aim for somewhere else ourselves. What's that other university called?"

At that point—I liked to think it might have been from residual Valdegeld pride—Mossa took control of the conversation again. "Can you tell us what your sister is like?" They stalled at this, with the usual confusion of youths being asked to describe someone they had known their whole lives, and she offered a prompt. "Was she as eager to get off Io as you are?"

"Oh yes," Nink, the younger brother, replied. "She couldn't stand it here."

"It's not Io," Laruch said quickly. "Or, not just Io. It's—our family, the other families, all this gunk about our heritage and lineage and—we all know who the real heroes were, the settlers who managed against all the challenges to move to a gas planet, not the ones who airlifted luxury Earth bunkers and buried them in the most seismically active orb in the galaxy."

I glanced involuntarily out the window at the tourist attraction, wondering if the kids had gotten all of this from novelas or books or if they had had a particularly pro-Giant governess.

"And your sister feels the same way?" Mossa asked.

"She's the one who told us all the stories about the settlers," the younger one said, eyes shining. That answered *that* question.

Mossa coaxed a few more facts out of them—Zebaia Elemaya's favorite foods, her inspiration for specializing in Speculative finance ("She always liked numbers, but playing with them, y'know?"), how she had seemed during her visit back between terms ("Normal, really."), and whether they had ever heard of Shaonam Strevan

("Who's that?"). She even persuaded them to let us read some of their sister's messages, molded into laminates sent with presents from the mainland.

"We never wanted to reconfigure them," Nink said sadly. "Even though we've got a machine." My eyes widened at the pride in his voice: *everyone* on Giant had a laminate shaper, or access to one.

"Buck up," Mossa told him. "She might well be back before you know it."

I wondered at her offering such speculative comfort, and asked once we were back in the vehicle. "It may be true," Mossa said, although her face was considerably grimmer than it had been as she spoke to the youths. "And it does no harm. In the meantime," she added, turning the buggy around for our return, "we seem to have found another character equally ripe for jumping the rails herself or being exploited by someone else."

Chapter 12

We did not have time to sleep before starting back for the shuttle port, and I was a little concerned about Mossa's ability to drive us without resting first.

"Truly, Pleiti, I'm able." Seeing my still skeptical expression, she shrugged, with a look of embarrassment. "In all honesty . . . I feel invigorated."

"By the investigation?" I could not see any cause for elation.

Mossa must not have either, because she wrinkled her nose. "No indeed! I suppose, if I must say . . . by being on my home ground again, I think. In any case I'm looking forward to the drive."

For a while we talked about Strevan and Elemaya, the personalities we traced in each and how our understanding of them had developed based on what we had learned on this trip. I must admit I dozed some on the way, but every time I opened my eyes, she was alert and observing; at least once she was speaking about the two missing students again, and I couldn't be sure whether she had waited for me to wake up to continue, or had been murmuring to herself the entire time, building the characters of her case in her mind. I had harbored a shameful hope that she would return with me, but from her ongoing, almost rail-of-consciousness chatter I gathered she planned to visit Strevan's school, both to learn more about his character and seek any evidence of intersections with Elemaya.

We arrived at the spaceport with an hour or so to spare before my embarkation. I told Mossa she needn't wait, fully expecting her to hurry off. The time on Io was limited, after all, and even my over-active yearning could not grudge her such rare opportunity to visit her—what was it?—*honorary aunties*—but she insisted that I eat before departing, and indeed I realized we hadn't had a proper meal in nearly a day.

Calculating that the least I could do was praise this place, obviously so much more important to her than I had assumed, I spent much of the gastronomic interval expounding on how fascinating I had found it, how beautiful. It was not a terrible strain to do so; indeed, when I realized how much I had spoken and how little she had, I began to wonder if I was rhapsodizing a bit too much. It was not until I had stood and was shouldering my satchel that Mossa told me to be careful. "I still don't have a good sense for the shape of this," she said. "But while these missing Ionians *may* not be connected to the others . . .

I cannot forget how very many people have disappeared from Valdegeld recently. Something is afoot, and we have made no secret of your involvement. That is to say . . . Pleiti, please don't go anywhere without letting me know, or leaving some message."

I was so startled by this unexpected evidence of concern that I could think of nothing appropriate, meaningful, or unique to say to her in return, and so stammered "Good-bye" as she walked off and then made my way to the shuttle, very alone. At least that frustration, and the enumeration of the many possible responses I could have made, distracted me through liftoff and half the flight.

The railcar journey home from Jaosou felt arduous, perhaps because I spent most of it berating myself for not appreciating my time on Io more, for not, in particular, showing Mossa how pleased I was to see her home. Yes, I had babbled about the place during that meal in the shuttle port, but had I made it clear that it only mattered to me because it mattered to her? The thought that she might class me as an ignorant tourist, seeing only the surface, was like a pang of acid in my throat. Or maybe she hadn't wanted me to see how much it mattered to her? Had she truly invited me only because of my fury on that previous occasion when she had tried to leave on a trip without me? Or was it about any hypothetical assistance I could provide with the investigation? Round and round on their immutable rings went my thoughts, as I stared at the endless fog.

I arrived home to find a laminate from the dean of Classics reminding me of my supposed obligation to attend the rector's memorial, which did not improve my mood. I noticed it would be held on Venusday, an unusual arrangement for a memorial; someone on the planning committee must have decided the more traditional Earthday would be too on the nose, which at least afforded me a snort of amusement. I tossed it into the reconfiguration chute and, after a quick bath and an unsatisfying grignoter of some bread and a boiled quail egg, fell into bed.

Chapter 13

I had fallen out of schedule in my travels, and woke at the wrong dawn, frowsy and flustered and immensely pleased to be home. My bed was smooth and cool, enveloping me with the sweetness of an ice-cream frappe; my rooms were quiet and mine alone; the heavier gravity a false but comforting assurance of safety. I lolled there, glorying in it, and at length realized there was no hope of falling back to sleep. I shook myself up and into some clothes and took a brisk walk around the neighborhood, a surprisingly bright morning and the colorful notices about the approaching Feast-Day further cheering me. I treated myself to a slapping breakfast at the poultry farm on the corner—they did a wonderful shakshouka, drizzled on fortunate days like that one with fresh yogurt from the milk of the goat they kept in the back—and ascended to my rooms for a proper pot of tea and a luxuriantly quiet morning reading, ready to concentrate on my own work for once.

It did not go well. In truth, I was finding it difficult, lately, to read about people leaping blithe and naked into bodies of water, or lying on swathes of grass, cradled in a co-evolved atmosphere. The mere mention of a horizon or of mud or of weeds was enough to clench my innards. These feelings were not unknown among Classical scholars, and I suppose we all had our ways of dealing with them; I told myself they would pass.

That malaise, which had been fogging me for a few weeks already, was only worsened by the persistent intrusions of thoughts of Mossa. I thought of her far more often than was my wont, even though it was hardly unusual for us to be apart for a few days; rather the norm in fact. I imagined her against the dramatic backdrop of Io, wondered if she regretted not living there. Was she working at that moment? Or relaxed and laughing, perhaps, with her peri-relatives? Was she thinking of me at all?

Perhaps my distraction was in part due to the way the circumstances were so reminiscent of the typical Modern love story: one of the lovers on a moon while the other(s) languished on Giant (in the stories, it was more common for the one on the moon to be languishing, but that was not my situation, and however much she was worried for my safety, I could not imagine it of Mossa). Was separation necessary for a romance? Were obstacles, real or illusory, a requirement? Was that why I could not feel satisfied when we were easy together (even if I was happier that way than when we were apart)? The earliest Modern love stories divided their personages between Giant and a spacecraft or space station (or sometimes on the same space station, separated into different compartments by terribly important procedures); then the moons came into play; and then, once Giant's settlements were sufficiently expanded, they could languish more conveniently on distant platforms, and other hindrances were needed to keep them separate besides the mere duration of a railcar journey.

Mossa managed to stay away often enough, even with only a short stretch of ring separating Sembla and Valdegeld.

At least Mossa was concerned about me, she had said so, and that was something; but of course she was, we were friends of long standing; we—she had said it herself—had a relationship of affection. Odder if she wasn't concerned about me. But then, there was concerned and there was concerned, just as there was caring about someone and caring, relationships and relationships, affection and—

I put the book away.

Perhaps working on the new Classical garden would cheer me. It would allow me to imagine, and perhaps eventually experience, at least a small part of Earth's so lauded *nature* here on Giant. I checked the hour: yes, I could get to the mauzooleum—the Koffre Institute for Earth Species Preservation—to consult with them about the necessary seeds and clippings, and be back with plenty of time to catch a nap and prepare for my tutorial. I grabbed an atmoscarf and my satchel and made for the train station.

My usual liaison at the Institute, a weedy and dedicated man named Ventresque, was off-shift since I had come on the wrong diurnal, but the garden project had been communicated generally and I had only little difficulty finding someone who could retrieve and package the first set of specimens for me and give me instructions for their reanimation and subsequent care. It was a simple errand, but between the physical movement and the sense of causing a tangible change in the world, I felt my mood start to buoy.

I plotted our route back to the Institute station so as to pass by my rabbits, the ones in the mini-biosphere designed based on my previous research project. I greeted the bunnies, without of course disturbing the experiment by anything so crass as sliding an extra carrot into the habitat, and then started towards the ring. On the way I noticed an enclosure that had been reconfigured; a new project. Such changes were not uncommon—the biospheres were designed to let scholars test particular combinations of species—but I spotted an unusual number of animals. "What project is *that* for?" My gaze darted about the area as I identified what I could: a mid-sized herbivore; a burrowing insectivore, which suggested there were insects, even if I couldn't see them from where I was; the flash of a hovering carnivore. It was rare to see so many pieces of an ecosystem together, most of us weren't so audacious, and the specific species were reminiscent of—

Understanding came on me in a flash, even as my escort hemmed evasively. "It's the rector's formula, isn't it?"

My guide nodded, reluctantly; they were probably trying to keep it quiet. "We put together the set that went in the rocket. This one we started right away; that one"—he gestured at an enclosure rather farther from the path—"is an effort to mimic the situation on Earth, and we tried to animate it roughly when the rocket—er, arrived." *Crashed*, he had been going to say.

"Do they know yet if . . ." I also stumbled. If the samples had been destroyed entering the atmosphere; if, surviving the crash, they had found Earth's remaining ecology hospitable enough to grow; if they would flourish temporarily, blocking our chances for a more scientific, enduring restart.

"Too soon," he said, a bit gruffly, and we went on our way.

I rode home in a mostly empty carriage with my eyes fixed on the fog. I did not want to think about the rector, or what might be happening on Earth, or if he had somehow been *right*. I tried to think about Mossa's case instead, and had a moment of eerie trompe l'oeil disorientation: for a moment it seemed frivolous to spend my time on a few missing people when, millions of miles away, the fate of humanity's homeland was being decided. I recovered, and persuaded myself that someone preying on students and employees of the university was far more important and immediate than the status of some faraway organisms.

What was Mossa learning on Io? (Would she transmit a message to update me? Or simply show up in my rooms again when she was back?) *Was* the disappearance of the two Ionians related to the larger pattern of missing people? I was not alone in the carriage, but I had a Valdegeld-trained memory, and was able to mentally rifle through the profiles that Mossa had collected. I fell into a sort of daze, watching the swirls of mist against the window, thinking through names and occupations, and in the back of my mind those two enclosures at the mauzooleum, that desperate attempt to cobble together something self-sustaining . . .

I blinked, coming wide awake as an idea solidified, and at almost the same moment the railcar slowed and the whistle blew for Valdegeld. Suddenly buzzing with energy, I disembarked and hurried to the heart of the Classics faculty, where I divested myself of the materials for the garden. Freed of that responsibility, I hesitated only long enough to check a laminate—yes, as I had recalled, Vecho Zei preferred to be in her kantor during the evenings, regardless of diurnal. She might not be there, of course, but I was not far from the Speculative campus. My tutorial was not until well after dawn in the next diurnal, and while I really ought to nap before then, sleep was unappealing at the moment. And perhaps I would learn something more about the missing Speculationists.

Chapter 14

I had to wait, pacing the corridor while the student in the office when I arrived and the two others queued in front of me paid obeisance in exchange for some academic favor or measured opinion. When I finally entered, fidgety with worry that erai dueña would be exhausted again, I found her patting at a trinity of succulents arranged on a draped altar below the single window. She seemed genki enough still, and unsurprised to see me, motioning me in with an elegant gesture and swinging the small kettle over the fire.

"Pleiti, isn't it?" Zei's acuity and retention were renowned, but even so I could not think she had my name tagged to my face. She had paid attention, of course, when Dean Mars had spoken to me the last time I visited. In all likelihood she had done her research on me since, and I tasted bile when I remembered the sort of chisme she was likely to hear about me these days. "I was sorry I didn't get a chance to converse with you last time you came. Utter foolishness, this business about memorializing Spandal."

I opened my mouth to join gleefully in his disparagement, then closed it. We had only so much time before some other supplicant entered, looking for a scrap of the dueña's time; I was there for data, not for vindication.

"I wanted to ask you, if I might, about some of the scholars in the Speculative faculty, and one of the students."

The kettle hummed and jittered, and Zei twitched the dial to lower the fire, then leaned forward to take the list of names I handed her. Her gaze flicked down the list, up it again, then to mine as she handed it back and reached for the teapot, canister, and strainer. "I haven't seen any of these people in some while." I was sure she had noticed the dates beside each name, corresponding to the day of referral to the Investigators or the last contact Mossa had been able to confirm. "These two." She pointed at the two from the Futures department. "My recollection is that they went to a conference in Stortellen, and when they did not return immediately it was assumed that they were taking some holiday, or perhaps had started a liaison." She raised her truncated arm such that I could almost see the non-existent fingers splaying in a gesture of ma'alesh, then reached for the kettle with her other arm, and poured the hot water into the teapot. "The others I did not know as well. And the student?"

"Name of Elemaya, in Speculative finance." Movement caught my eye: a hearth snake twined around the gas pipe detached itself and slithered down to the warm stones just under the coil.

"Is she gone too? That's a shame. An intelligent child. Very proud."

"Proud?"

"Of herself, of her place. You know the type: not willing to hear a word of Giant's superiority over Io." *Did* I know the type? Mossa certainly chafed a bit at the way people talked about Io, but was she proud of her home?

"Sounds more resentful than proud," I heard myself say. I wondered at it too; the interview with her family had not given me the impression that she was a dissonant patriot.

Zei considered. "Hmm. Perhaps a little. It was more a kind of determination, I think, a resistance to the dominant narrative that Giant is better, as opposed to a plumped-up belief in Io."

While she poured the tea, a quote from Mossa's interview notes about Strevan came to my mind: *He arrived here thrilled and admiring, everything was the greatest of the good, Valdegeld had no wrong to it, and then, naturally, the weight crushed the pedestal and he was furious at it for not living up to his illusions.*

"Mmm," I said, lifting my cup to inhale the aroma. I thought I had heard a shuffling in the corridor outside the door, but now that the tea was poured I felt I had that at least as a bulwark against interruptions. I would drink slowly and try to keep her talking. "There are a number of people like that here, and not only from Io."

"Indeed." Her eyes strayed again to the list, which I

still had on my lap. "Elemaya worked for the bursar, you know. I believe she had some fairly radical opinions, but to be a practicum with that man she must have kept them well to herself." Zei lifted a small saucer in my direction. "Chapulín cake?"

I took one, intending to nibble infinitesimally; Zei broke hers, tossing half in her mouth and holding out the other half to the snake by the fire, which condescended to accept it. "I will say, recently I have had cause to wonder . . ." I held my breath around the delicate anise flavor of the cake, waiting to hear what she had wondered.

"There are others missing," I said when she didn't continue, hoping to bring her into the urgency of it, hoping I wasn't being indiscreet. "This is only those connected with the Speculative faculty, but if you have any suspicions, the matter may indeed be urgent." Zei appeared to be fascinated by the inside of her teacup, and I tried to remember what we had been talking about. "The bursary? The funding of this faculty . . ."

"Oh, I don't know these things," Zei said, suddenly impatient.

And yet, she had wondered something. I waited, and waited, parsing out my tea like the last unread book. The dueña's eyelids lowered, then raised: A wink? A hint? Or somnolence? She stroked the underside of the snake's chin; I resisted the final swallow of tea.

At last Zei raised her teacup to look at me over its rim, almost coquettish. "I know nothing about these others. It may have nothing to do with them. But Elemaya . . ." I could hear my teeth grinding during the pause. "She seemed a worthwhile student, a decent person. I have recently become somewhat . . . suspicious may be too strong a word." She appraised me. "You are not in the Speculative faculty, I don't know if you're aware of some of the dynamics involved in the, ah, the development of prototypes."

I frowned.

"Ah, some are supported by the university directly; others by other investors, and under certain conditions those funds spill over into university coffers; some are joint ventures; others completely self-funded, or apparently so until they are shown to be viable. It is complicated, and there are incentives, you understand."

"But that is, if I'm not wrong, the normal state of things in this faculty." I had heard about the fraught elbowing for development opportunities. "You suggested something has changed to raise your concerns recently."

Zei raised her cup a fraction in my direction. "It has always been . . . precariously balanced, shall we say; dependent, like so many supposed systems, on the personalities involved. And their principles." She put down her cup, turned it a quarter-rotation widdershins. "Something is off. Or, perhaps, the balance has shifted for entirely legitimate reasons but . . . my gut," she pounded her midsection with the stump of her arm, "suspects some shiftiness there."

I wondered if she simply disliked the bursar. "Do you connect that to any of these names?"

Zei raised her arm again. "Elemaya worked with the bursar, an appropriate place for mismanaging funds. That is the only connection I see, and perhaps it is an imagined one. Although then again, these scholars . . . if you were putting together a team to develop something new, you might expect to see a grouping of specializations like this one. Perhaps a prototype went wrong, or went too well . . ."

I could almost hear the snap of synapses as the connection was made; what Zei had said mirrored my partial, exhaustion-blurred insight on the way back from the mauzooleum.

"Well." I said it slowly, not wanting to show my excitement, but when I glanced up Zei was watching me closely, a half smile on her lips. My cup was, in any case, empty, and the shuffling outside the door had already manifested a timid knock. "Thank you, Dueña Zei, you've been so kind with your time."

Chapter 15

I sauntered out of the hall, full of elation at having made a connection that might explain the unusual grouping—porters, porters were almost all former railworkers, they certainly had useful skills; and Modern engineers, like Strevan, and Speculationists; few or no Classicists on the list, which I tried not to be offended by, although I knew Mossa would be amused . . .

I paused. Mossa would not be at my rooms that night (to my knowledge at least—the misguided hope of a surprise visit made my heart ache) and my epiphany lost quite a bit of its sparkle if I could not share it with her. Frustrated, I glanced around the darkening plaza, and decided on impulse to visit the bursar of the Speculative faculty.

The bursary was in the next building along the plaza,

past a crèche and a dining hall and a handball center and up a winding ramp and down a long corridor; further delayed by the layers of office staff, I only just got in to see him before closing, and while he was polite he made no effort to answer in any way that would extend his working time. Yes, Elemaya had worked in his office, as many students did every term; she had a particular specialization in large organizational finances, and had been extremely helpful; he couldn't speak to her academic endeavors, but from his perspective he certainly would have recommended her anywhere, when it came to that, but he thought she still had another year at least? Yes, he had heard she was not to be located at the moment, but it had only been a few days, all right then, nearly a week perhaps; this was not so uncommon with students, and he was still hoping she would return. Strevan he didn't know.

I emerged into the night, blinking and unsatisfied. Perhaps Zei had been indulging in a bit of academic spite, revenging herself on the bursar for reasons good or bad, or perhaps simple petty dislike. Or perhaps her instincts were correct but unrelated to my investigations, or perhaps I simply lacked the knowledge and access to find the clue I needed to understand.

My rooms held no appeal whatsoever, but I was wrinkling my nose and resigning myself—and wondering whether it was worth attempting to convey my suppositions in a telegram to Io—when I was hailed from the entrance of the building whence I had just come. Through the (rather flash) gauzed atmoscarf I recognized one of the office staff who had moderated my admittance to the bursar's office. "Yes?" I said, my heartbeat quickening.

"Sorry about him," he said, nodding back up in clear reference to the bursar. "He's annoyed she hasn't come in, and all the more irritated because he doesn't have the chisme on it."

And you do? was ready formed in my mouth, but I kept it in, responding only with a nod. The staffer—a student almost certainly, working there like Elemaya as part of his training—did not seem in any hurry to walk on, so I settled beside him in the entrance arch of the building, out of the drizzle that had started misting the plaza.

"I'm a little worried about Elemaya, to be honest," the young man said. "She's probably fine, I know she had talked about seeing more of Giant, but . . . I think she would have spoken of a trip, if she were planning one. And then you mentioned Strevan. He's missing too?"

I nodded again, with confirmation this time.

"Maybe they went off together then. Might be a bit more spontaneous that way." The staffer scoffed. "I heard himself telling you he didn't know Strevan, but he's certainly seen him before, was in and out of here a bunch."

"To see Elemaya?" I asked, wanting to be sure.

The staffer scowled. "And others, he had a bunch of mates here. I think he might have been regretting the choice of Modern, to be honest."

I was trying to figure out how to work the conversation around to the possible financial mismanagement Zei had suggested without either offending my informant or putting his position in danger when he went on. "Didn't think much of him myself. Always bragging or wheedling or looking sly. He was a Cat, you know."

I blinked, then blinked again as I understood the implied capital letter. "Who, Strevan?"

The staffer nodded.

"*Really.*" That hadn't been in Mossa's dossier, but now that I thought about it, it wasn't so surprising. The oldest and most traditional club of Valdegeld was called the Pigeons; it had been established shortly after the successful reanimation and introduction of that fowl on Giant, and it must have seemed a name both eminently Classical and celebratory of the biotechnical future. There were several other clubs of around the same vintage, but the Cat had come along a generation or two later. The name was definitely aimed at the Pigeons, and intended to hint at troublemaking along the lines of the old adage. It was just the place for someone furious at Valdegeld while still enamored of the romantic dream of a scholar's life.

"Liked to invite people there, or hint at how he could. Thought it was quite impressive." He sniffed, and I spared a thought for the telenovela's worth of office rivalries, aspirations, entanglements, and intrigues that Elemaya and Strevan had left untethered when they disappeared. "I keep trying to think," the staffer went on, his eyes gliding along the Speculative artwork, the building façades behind me, "trying to remember: When was the last time I saw her, what did she say? But it's all just sort of . . . blended together and, yeah." He sniffed again, this time with less annoyance and more emotion. "Rabbit horns, I hope you find her."

"I hope so too," I said. "Please let me know if you do remember anything, but—don't beat yourself up over it, all right? You couldn't have known."

He nodded, and with a quick farewell plunged into the thickening rain. I hesitated another moment under the overhang of the entrance, but if I hadn't wanted to go home before, I certainly wasn't going to now. Besides, it was past midnight, the perfect time to delve into Valdegeld's nightlife.

Chapter 16

Verilo Road was not quite the heave of Valdegeld's club and theater district, but nor was it too far, a quick walk to Sessiranaib Avenue but even closer to Valdegeld's third and smallest railcar station, with just a touch of its seediness. The Cat Club overlooked the street from its somewhat bulbous, tall building, rather awkwardly caught between hewing to the tradition that was, really, its only claim to eliteness, while not falling too far out of date. In that, of course, it was much like all the clubs; the Cat had something of an advantage in that it had *always* had the role of the outsider to a certain extent: the club that laughed quietly in its sleeve about all the other clubs and even just a little about itself. Still, in my circles at least the joke felt a bit stale, and I had never before visited the place.

The foyer was from an era when it had been popular to mimic the even older practice of building residences that doubled as escape pods, and it had that conical, compact look to it, although I was fairly certain it did not actually have the capacity for liftoff. There was a dim sort of smell to the air, as though they didn't clean often enough, which I supposed wasn't surprising. There were plenty of people who would clean up after university students, for an ample consideration; very few, however, were willing to clean up after them *and* treat them as superiors. Most positions in the student clubs were therefore, as I understood it, either held by the students themselves on a rotating basis or by alums.

(This was not true of all of them; contrary to commonly accepted belief, there are enough non-students in Valdegeld for some non-student institutions to thrive. I myself harbored hopes of someday joining the Hecuba Club, whose membership was preponderantly adult and interested in the theater: a place to be in company with other aficionados and in particular to dine before shows, since its restaurant was carefully calibrated to perfect the logistics of eating at leisure without missing curtain time.)

The young man at the Cat Club reception, however, was clearly a student, and blanched when I asked about Strevan. "Oh, radiation, are you his tutor? Because whatever he's done, I'm sure it's just a jaunt, no need to get all serious about it."

"Is he here then?" I asked, without much hope.

"Possibly?" the boy equivocated, drawing out the

vowels improbably. "He has a room he uses here some-times, I don't know if he's in . . ." He trailed off at my star-tled gape.

"Let's have a look," I said, recovering myself enough to hold out my hand with the combination of imperiousness and camaraderie typical of young tutors who don't wish to be hated: a bit of authority, but also *one of you.*

"Well, I . . . shouldn't . . ." His eyes darted about the room as though looking for an escape; if there *had* been an ejectable pod, I felt sure he would have triggered it. Following his gaze I noticed for the first time the tabby lying, as if this were acceptable, on an armchair; an epon-ymy thing, I supposed.

"You certainly should. He's late for tutorial."

"It's just, we've a policy of privacy and"—he quailed visibly under my glare—"Strevan himself, he's very par-ticular about not being disturbed."

Another cat came to the internal doorway, paused there tail a-twitch, and then without hurry retreated the way it had come. Belatedly, I connected the felines with the fug I had noticed in the air.

"He's *eight days* late for tutorial," I said sternly. My initial rush of hopefulness at imagining that Strevan might be so easily found had given way to a more realistic foreboding: he might well enough be in his room, but I couldn't imagine he was in very good shape if he was. I swallowed against the image, and when I spoke again my voice was gentler than I had intended. "What if he's taken ill, or incapacitated? Come on, we have to check."

I chivvied the boy—I couldn't countenance calling

him an adult—from the reception, reminded him to fetch the key from its hook, reminded myself to ask his name, which was Norzin. Whether from nerves or a natural garrulousness, he proceeded to inform me, without being asked, that he was a student in Modern architecture but was thinking about switching to Speculative, it had more *scope,* in his phrasing, and that he was from Tiester. "Long way to come," I commented, distractedly worrying whether, if someone *was* preying on isolated students, he might be next. At that moment I was too concentrated on Strevan's status to attempt that discussion (and how would it go? *Be wary of anyone trying to take advantage of you* generally went down a treat with overly young, insufficiently secure provincials).

In any case we had, via a number of narrow passages and stairs, reached the door. Norzin managed to open it with only slight fumbling, and we found the room empty. I checked the closet and under the bed to be certain, noting that the Cat's alleged luxury did not go very deep, and then we returned, relieved but pensive (at least on my part), to the foyer.

"Sorry we couldn't be of assistance." Norzin was smiling, probably from relief that he had managed to avoid my anger without betraying one of his club mates. "I'll certainly tell him you stopped by if I should see him."

"Eight days late for tutorial," I reminded him, trying to impress the gravity of the situation on that malleable cognition. "Nobody's seen him for ten. Do you have any idea where he might be?"

Norzin appeared to think about it, then demurred. "I

don't know him that well, never really seen him outside of the Cat."

I cast an involuntary glance at one of the specimens lolling nearby and controlled a shudder. "Do you know anyone who does know him well?"

His smile turned bland: he certainly did not want to reveal the members' friendships.

I had another idea. "Do you have a registry? Of guests, I mean?"

Nodding eagerly, he reached under the desk to fetch it. I wondered how many more requests he would respond to before it occurred to him I had no real standing or authority. I was still considering whether I would dare, or even want, to invoke the Investigators when my running finger stopped at Strevan's name and, just below it, Elemaya's.

They had lunched here. Together. Ten days ago, and no one had seen him since.

My pulse was pounding. "Were you here when he brought a guest for lunch, a bit over a week ago?" I turned the registry to show him, in case it might chug his memory along, but he still took an unreasonably long time to think and calculate.

"I was," he admitted at last, "but I can't say I remember much of it. Had a bad head that day if I recall correctly. Anyhap those two have eaten here a few times, they sort of blend together. Not the two of them, obviously, the memories, I mean."

"But you don't remember if—you don't remember anything about how they were that day?"

Norzin wandered internally for a while again, then shook his head regretfully.

"Might someone else?"

He checked the schedule, still unwavering in his belief in me, but the server from that day was not in the club at the moment. I told myself to go home, that the practical thing would be to leave at that point. Several students had come past us while we spoke, there was a murmur of noise from the rooms above that was sure to swell soon. They would be busy; I was tired; I had learned all I reasonably could.

And yet. If I left, I might not find another so accommodating informant when I returned; it might occur to even this young man to be suspicious in the interim. More than that, I was held in curiosity's gravity, or maybe in speculation's: I could not let it go. I was by then feeling distinctly queasy, and if Mossa had been on the same celestial sphere, I would have gladly handed it over, or at the least telegraphed and waited for her to arrive, but she wasn't.

It had been days, and no one had noticed, so if my uneasy suspicions had any basis, I would need to look for someplace cold. "Could I see your kitchens?"

I emerged from the kitchen areas with a firm conviction that I would never willingly eat at the Cat Club, but the dubious sanitation did not extend to the point of corpses. I started for the door, not without a feeling of relief, and then stopped. "The, er, the roof," I said, dread growing on me as I said it. "Is there a pocket in the atmoshield, do you know?" The boy looked at me blankly.

"The roof," I all but snarled, feeling a sudden kinship to Mossa in her more irascible moods. "Where is the access to the roof?"

He showed me. I thought he might follow me up the narrow staircase, and both wanted a witness and didn't, but he was hailed from one of the rooms we passed, and darted away with assurances of his quick return. At that moment I discovered that I definitively did not want a witness, for I hurried up the stairs as quickly as I could and pushed open the trapdoor with a sense of escape.

Many buildings with roofs close to the atmoshield took advantage of the extra, chilled storage space by building small cupboards or closets, colloquially known as *pockets,* into the thinner, frigid air. This one was just a kind of wooden rack with a grate. I could see immediately that there was something there, as I had both expected and disbelieved, but I had to walk right up to those suspended wooden bars before I could be certain that the corpse inside belonged to Strevan.

Chapter 17

I insisted that they wire Mossa immediately. I insisted on this at length, with a fervor that would once have been attributed to a displacement in my internal organs, and to everyone I saw: to poor Norzin, whom I suspected would recall this experience, too, as involving a bad headache; to the university representative, a tweedy scholar who was the first person Norzin alerted; eventually, to the local Investigators. I kept insisting even after these last had assured me it would be done, even after they assured me it *had* been done, unwilling to believe until I had proof in the form of the reply.

It was fortunate for me, if somewhat embarrassing once I eventually grokked it, that one of the local Investigators who responded was one I had encountered, if not formally met, in Mossa's company during our previous investigation. It was recognizing her that brought me somewhat back to myself, or perhaps I only recognized her once I began to calm, but in any case she was sitting beside me and my hands were wrapped around a cooling mug. I brought it automatically to my mouth, and almost choked: the tea was over-sweet.

"That's better then," the Investigator said, soothingly, and I had the feeling she'd been speaking to me in that tone for some time. "Nice and easy."

I took a breath that shuddered excessively, but when I tried my voice it was mostly clear. "Have I made much of a fool of myself?"

"Not at all," she said, meaning *yes very much*. "You did exactly the right thing. Contacted us—"

I felt, or imagined, a note of reproach there, and protested that I had *told* Norzin to send for the Investigators *before* the university, and she shushed me and went on. "Contacted us, as I said; wouldn't let anyone else near the body, and apprised us of our colleague's existing connection with the situation." She smiled at me reassuringly, and I felt a little better.

"I, er, I don't believe we were introduced when we met before. Pleiti Weihal."

"Nervil. Aigho Nervil. Shall we get you home?"

I looked around the foyer. It was true, the chairs were uncomfortable and I disliked the tea—I shuddered with the thought that it had probably been stewed in that horrible kitchen—but—

"No reply from Mossa yet?"

"Not yet, but you know how Io is. If she was anywhere

outside of Morabito she might not even have gotten the message yet. Even in Morabito they're not terribly rushed with telegram deliveries, I've heard. We'll make sure any reply is brought to you directly—if, that is, she doesn't think to send it directly to your rooms instead, and wouldn't that be like her? Perhaps it's already there."

With such soothing statements she shepherded me finally out of the repellent Cat Club and down streets that were now brightening (and I was going to get off schedule again, wasn't I?) and, in that part of town, crowded with revelers on their way home or pressing on to another desperate entertainment. I did manage to convince her to leave me at the porter's lodge, once Genja had confirmed that there was no message, and I got myself up the stairs.

I took the requisite very hot bath, pretending that external cleanliness would provide some similar disinfection of the mind and the horrified memory. Following that partial remedy I self-medicated with hot tea—very hot, maintained by ordering more pots, in quicker succession, than I would normally have allowed myself—cushions, blankets, and a compilation of the most comforting music I knew. And then I waited.

Waiting was not enough to stave off memories of Strevan's father and that desperate hole where he lived, his bathetic misunderstandings of his son and misapprehensions of Valdegeld. I imagined how he was told, his grief, went so far as to design an entire organization for providing assistance to indigent Ionian families. Unable to sleep, I had been driven to reading—not my academic work, but a rather frivolous yet skilled Modern novel—before the knock came and Nakalo, Genja's successor in the porter's lodge that day, handed me the telegram.

WELL DONE STOP OMW M

Those few words proved sufficient to distract me for some time. *Omw* was an archaism, a Classical expression meaning she was coming back; I spent an inordinate amount of time wondering whether Mossa would have used that expression with, say, one of her Investigator colleagues or whether it was a nod at my interests. After some time I understood that this was a ridiculous question and indicative of exhaustion, and I went to bed.

Chapter 18

I had completely missed my scheduled tutorial; when I finally woke up enough to realize this, I sent an apology and managed to gather myself for a rescheduled session that I attended but afterwards had no memory of. I went to Soyal Courtyard to plant some of the seeds I had collected the day before, which helped a bit, feeling the soil crumble around my fingers. Afterwards I returned to my rooms, poked at my reading but did not absorb it, and generally stared at the wall. A plainly covered laminate arrived from the Investigators' office, with a note saying that Mossa had requested I be sent the preliminary results; even wondering *results of what* did not inspire enough curiosity for me to open it.

Finally, rather late at night (and, well I knew, at almost the earliest point she could possibly have been expected), and fortuitously to the strains of one of my favorite arias, Mossa flung open the door. "Pleiti!"

I suspect she had some more jocular greeting on her lips, but she saw my face, or posture perhaps, and squelched it. "Pleiti? Dearest, are you well?"

The word *dearest* was, undoubtedly, an exaggeration, a meaningless verbal tic. Perhaps it was a cultural characteristic of Io to exaggerate affection in the vocative (though I had not noticed it while I was there). Whatever the reason, it shocked me enough to crack the numbness surrounding me, and I surfaced into my emotions like someone taking a breath after diving underwater.

"Mossa!" I pushed to my feet and threw my arms around her.

I was subsumed in the comfort of her warmth, her solidity and presence, her *self*, brilliant and alert. I was not fully conscious of anything else during the first few moments of that embrace, anything beyond those sensations, but when my awareness unfurled again she was holding me, as solid as I could desire; and, more, her voice was whispery, her breath soft on my cheek: "Pleiti," she murmured, and I am sure she stroked my hair. "Oh Pleiti, I'm so sorry." *Sorry* was not what I had wanted to hear (and what was? *I missed you so, I'm so fond of you, I'm so yearning, I'm ravie to be back with you, I'm so in . . .*) but even so I leaned in closer for another moment before disengaging. I swiped at my eyes, but what I saw of her face in between was, indeed, pitying. "It must have been awful, I'm sorry, I should have come back sooner."

"It—" I could not say *It wasn't so bad,* because even

the most cursory attempt at truthfulness would have required reliving that moment of recognizing the carcase, and I wasn't ready to risk it. "I'll do. Thank you for coming back so quickly." Already, I could feel resentment creeping, that she thought me so weak as to be overturned by a single corpse.

"I cannot believe I wasn't closer to hand," she responded, starting to pace. "I was worried about you, you know, when you left, I thought—I'm happy nothing worse happened."

Was I melting or angry, or both? I couldn't tell—when had I last slept, really slept?—so I said the first kind sentence I could find: "I missed you."

Mossa turned towards me and smiled, like a hearth flooding into warmth when the fire was ignited. "And I you, Pleiti! Would that you could have stayed with me!"

"I'm sorry," I said, with some difficulty. "I'm sorry I left, sorry that I dragged you back here before you had finished your—your visit."

"You can hardly be blamed for that, Pleiti. And as for your leaving, you have your responsibilities."

"Yes, well," I said, ruefully—I was more than ready by then to put overblown emotions aside—"I might well have stayed for the attention I've been able to put to my studies the past few days."

"Indeed, you've been doing my work instead, solving the case without me."

I snorted, then had to fight a yawn. "Hardly," I managed. "Made it worse, more like."

"Not at all," Mossa said, eyeing me. "Pleiti, when did

you last eat? No idea? I thought not. Let me put in an order and then—will you tell me how you came to visit the Cat Club?"

Over a thick, reassuringly spiced lentil stew I told her.

"Hmm. Interesting that no one I spoke to had mentioned his membership there."

"From what the bursary staffer told me, it was something he liked to flaunt, but he may have been canny enough to choose only appreciative targets." I smothered another yawn; with the warmth of the stew in my belly I was fighting off slumber, but Mossa had noticed the laminate that had come from the Investigators.

Wiping her fingers fastidiously she picked it up, turned it in her hands, and, inevitably, noted that I hadn't opened it. "Pleiti? You haven't—ah." Just as inevitably she drew her conclusions, but without belaboring she cracked the seal herself and settled in to examine it. I fiddled with the edge of the blanket until, finished, she passed it to me without asking whether I would like to read it.

"Stabbed," she said, conversationally, as I was still trying to decide whether I wanted that information in my brain. "The weapon is gone, but there's an interesting diagram positing what its business end looked like." Resigned, I started reading, missing most of what Mossa soliloquized in the interim—on the assumption that she was continuing to summarize the data in the brief—until my mind insisted I pay attention: "—lucky the cats didn't get to him. I imagine they don't like the cold up there."

"Really, Mossa!" I looked up sharply and saw the littlest of her smiles. "Very well," I huffed. "Very well, I'm back with you. Do you think it was Elemaya who killed him after their lunch?"

"Their lunch?" It was her turn to snap to attention, and I realized that I hadn't pointed out the guestbook to the Investigators; I would have assumed that they would check it on their own, but perhaps they hadn't realized the significance of the name, or maybe they had only sent their findings on the body and any further reporting would follow. I explained what I had learned from the callow receptionist, and then had to go back and outline, in detail, everything else I had done since returning from the moon.

"You must be tired, after the journey," I ventured at last, when she hadn't spoken in some time.

She waved her hand negligently. "Not to speak of. But the storyline we are following"—still *we,* I noticed—"has taken some unexpected twists. I need to think. I doubt I will be able to sleep yet, but you should go ahead."

With a murmured word or two I retired to my bed. Only the wish that she was in it with me delayed my sleep, and even that not for very long.

Chapter 19

Mossa remained largely immobile for the next day and most of the following, acurrucada in a nest of cushions in front of the fire while I followed the necessary rituals of my job. When I hurried out to my tutorial on the first day I assumed that she would feed herself; seeing no evidence on my return that this had happened, I ordered a tray of empanadas and left it beside her, and was gratified to see her eat the entire tray with an aspect of distraction.

On the second day I betook myself to my office to meet with a student, and then to the library, but I found myself pausing often in my reading and calculations. The horror of finding the body had by then faded somewhat, and I found I was eager for the chase: *someone* had done that to that poor student, and it could not stand. And what did it bode for the other disappeared? I hurried back from the library, ready to urge Mossa to action, and was therefore doubly pleased to see her standing in front of my wall, which she had turned into a storyboard. Divested of my accoutrements, I went to stand beside her.

"Any advance?"

Mossa, usually so contained, turned away from the wall with a frustrated flick of her arms. "Distressing."

I eyed the storyboard in some alarm. "Er . . ."

Mossa threw herself on the chaise. "You must see, Pleiti, how unsatisfying is the state of the data at this point. There *must* be some gaps, despite all the information we have found—"

I raised my hand to forestall her. "Has there been additional information since we last spoke of it?" One of the things that had occurred to me at the library was that a day and a half seemed a long time to go without updates, if the Investigators were examining the Cat Club site at all.

Mossa blinked at me. "When *did* we last speak properly? Hmm, has it been so long? Well then."

Seeing her settle herself, and being still chilled from my walk home, I rang for tea and scones. Warm and comfortable, sipping and nibbling while she talked, nodding as she told me her theories, I felt an unexpected flow of domestic contentment, a sense of comfort which I couldn't help but mistrust.

". . . looked into their movements after that suspicious luncheon, naturally," Mossa was saying, and I was nodding, as though it were perfectly normal for her to be telling me about a murder investigation. "Both Elemaya and

Strevan were seen leaving the Cat Club after their meal. They walked off together; perhaps he was accompanying her somewhere, or perhaps he had an errand in the same direction as her next destination." And maybe it *was* normal. She was recounting her day at work, after all. "It is thought that he returned, although the certitude is lower than I would like: another member who thinks he saw him there that afternoon, but can't be quite sure of the date, spending as he does his every day dissipated there."

But Mossa would not tell me something in order to unload its emotional import, much less merely to hear herself talk. She was not telling me about her day at work in the sense of sharing what was important to her or filling the silence or trying to hold my interest or because she thought I owed her my interest (a litany inspired by comparing the interpreted motives of other people who had, in the past, thought fit to tell me about their days on a regular basis). She was telling me because she believed I would be helpful. "And then that evening he commanded dinner to his room, although the person who brought it did not see him, knocking and leaving it outside the door."

"There was no tray or dinner service in the room when I looked," I said, drawn out of my introspection. "I would have noticed the smell at the very least."

"Mmm, the staff confirmed that. So far we haven't found anyone working there who remembers removing the tray from the hallway, so we don't know whether the food was eaten or not."

"Or by whom," I murmured.

"Indeed. Now, it is of course possible that Elemaya returned to the club so as to attack Strevan in his room after their lunch, which was described by the server as being somewhat contentious, but not overly heated. She could easily have done so without being noticed I think?"

I nodded, wrinkling my nose in dissatisfaction. "Easily, but just as easily anyone else could have. The guestbook is pure theater, meant to impress people who are invited for meals; in the evenings anyone can walk in."

"Or out," Mossa noted.

"But what about the other missing," I cried, no longer able to bottle my concern. "Seventeen people! Have you given up on them? Do you think they all met a similar fate?"

Without looking, Mossa swept her arm at the storyboard behind her, where indeed the other dossiers hung, suspended in uncertainty around the margins. "Down to sixteen now—no, not because of Strevan." She tossed me a flimsy from the Investigators; one of the missing students had been located on Zaohui, having apparently decided to transfer to the university there while neglecting to fill in any paperwork to that effect. "But the others! See here, Pleiti—you found the body on a hunch, an inspired one, but even so, it was not a very secure hiding place."

"It wasn't!" Somehow, in the shock of it, that hadn't occurred to me. "Even from the door to the roof, I could see that there was something—something *wrong* in the atmoshield pocket." A chill swirled over my skin.

"Someone would have noticed eventually, probably sooner rather than later." Mossa paused, waiting.

"None of the other bodies have been found." I did not want to follow this ring of thought.

"So either this is an outlier, or—"

"Or the murderer was planning to move the body and hadn't managed it yet." The chill became a full-body shudder. What if the murderer had been waiting there, in the club, *or even on the roof*? What if they had been watching me?

"I think the latter unlikely, however," Mossa said dispassionately. "After all, it has been some time since Strevan was killed. Surely if getting rid of the body was important to them, they would have found a time to do it."

"Or maybe it's completely unconnected." I gazed at the storyboard, wondering why I was so reluctant to accept separating the murder from the disappearances. "You would still investigate the missing people, wouldn't you?"

The pause was a little too long. "As far as I am able."

That was why. Without the murder and the more recent disappearances, the missing lost their urgency. On Giant, it was too easy for people to disappear. "They don't even fit in the storyboard," I said, exhaustion and sorrow leaching despondence into my tone.

Mossa didn't seem to hear it; she had swiveled in her chair to study the storyboard. "Do you know, Pleiti," she said, after some time, "I believe you're right?"

It was only a statement of fact, not even real praise, and I fought against how it lifted the worst of my melancholy. Then she went on: "I'm going to need to cut them out to see the shape of it."

I sat up straight. "Don't!"

"I will investigate, Pleiti," she said, too gently. "I won't forget them. But perhaps in their own storyboard—collectively or separately—"

"Collectively." I had remembered, in a flash, the idea that had come to me—how many days ago had it been now?—before evaporating with the shock of the corpse. "Mossa. What if it's not how they're similar that's important, but how they're different?" She was frowning at me intently. "What if it's a—" I could not say *ecosystem*, it felt too similar to our previous investigation and too far-fetched at the same time. "What if they're meant to be filling different niches—that is, different needs?" I leapt to my feet and began pointing at the dossiers pinned to my wall. "Vecho Zei said something to me about the specializations looking like a project team, but it would have to be something a bit more than that, something more comprehensive. Look: People who know how to cook. People who know how to build, and engineers, and electrical specialists. People who know the rails!"

"Pleiti!" Mossa stood up too, began to pace, staring at the wall. "It could be . . . it could be, Pleiti!" A full smile had spread across her face, and in that moment I could not have been prouder if she had awarded me the Scholar's Ribbon then and there. She did not, however, stop pacing. "Self-sufficiency," she muttered. "Isolation? Surely . . . but there must be some driving force . . ." She went on along that rail for some time, no longer talking to me, or even, I think, aware of me. I sat down again and watched the fire for a time, my elation fading, and finally roused myself to suggest, without much hope for it, that we venture out for supper. I had to suggest it three times, in point of fact, before Mossa blinked at me in surprise.

"I'd prefer to eat here, if you don't mind, Pleiti. You've given me much to think about."

I found, as I went to order, that I was repressing not only a sigh, but a smile, and was startled at myself: if I found her puzzle-solving moods endearing, I was far gone indeed.

Chapter 20

The next morning Mossa was once again cocooned by the fire, and when she responded only absently to my cautious overtures I set off determinedly for my office.

I did not, however, get very much work done. I was at that time analyzing an account, supposedly truthful although I found some of it frankly unbelievable, of a small-town doctor. The plant and animal species mentioned were strictly background, bits of scenery that the (rather pompous) narrator mentioned to add color or because his editor told him to—I put down the book, aware that my irritation was impeding my focus. And what was the point, anyway? There I was, in my tiny carrel in a building full of trained scholars, all of us teasing out minutiae of evidence day after day in hopes of approximating in the incomprehensible complexity of our lost ecosystems, and meanwhile—

Meanwhile, on Earth, the rector's haphazard collection might even now be taking root.

The image of those infinitesimal cells sending out tendrils of life struck me with a squirming mix of anguish and terrified hope. Such sprouts might, as I had told the rector, generate an unbalanced ecosystem, not viable in the long term and complicating our more considered efforts, pushing back any possibility of resettlement for generations. Or *what if the rector was right*? What if Earth was already survivable, what if his absurd ecosystem *worked*? *What if we could go back?*

What if with all our care and academic rigor we were only making things harder for ourselves, and to no purpose?

I wanted to wire the mauzooleum to ask how their mock-up was doing, or even catch a railcar there to see for myself, offer my assistance, which was ridiculous because I had a job. My expertise was in textual analysis, not the care and feeding of extinct species. Instead, I turned my thinking to the disappeared. Deciding that I might as well get *something* done that day, I gathered my things and exited into the chilly air.

My hopes of a breakthrough, or even measurable progress, did not come to fruition, but not for lack of trying. I went first back to the Speculative bursary, hoping to get more information about the projects Elemaya had worked on or perhaps more gossip about Strevan, but the staffer I had spoken to previously wasn't on shift and nobody else seemed to have an opinion on Strevan. I had remembered

Vecho Zei's comment about a prototype "that failed, or did too well," but (the bursar's assistant told me) Elemaya had done generalized assistance rather than leading on any discrete projects, and gentle prodding yielded nothing further. I went from there to the Speculative faculty registrar, in an attempt to learn what I could about the other missing, and from there to the registrar of the Modern faculty, but I gleaned nothing that was not already in Mossa's dossiers. Feeling useless, I changed tack entirely and turned my steps towards my own faculty and Soyal Courtyard.

Between myself, the Classical botanist, and the Modern agriculturalist who had been appointed to the squadron, we had planted most of that initial haul of specimens, but there were a few left to sow still. The others weren't around that evening, and I worked quietly on my own, occasionally sitting back on my heels to appreciate the quiet beauty of the spot. As usual, the tactile tasks calmed me. I found myself humming under my breath—the second aria of *Murderbot*. Though it was cold, it was clear, and I looked up every so often to admire the moons reflected in the façade of the Silvered Library, one of the buildings surrounding the courtyard. (That was not its official name, of course. When Valdegeld was founded, the committee took a strong stance against the Classical tradition of so-called academic indulgences: naming buildings, departments, jobs, et cetera after individuals in exchange for funds. Therefore, all official Valdegeld buildings were namkaraned through a process of randomized phonemes (with certain veto options). The

Trisklan Library, however, was widely called the Silvered Library in reference to the particularly shiny metal of its superstructure.)

I was once again appreciating the view—and beginning to think about heading back to my rooms—when I saw the reflection of Ganymede shiver. It gave me a moment of vertigo, as I wondered whether the platform I stood on was vibrating, but fortunately I was not so distracted by my puzzlement not to notice when the plate on the side of the building loosed and began to slide downwards, gathering speed as it slipped towards me. I gaped for almost too long, then threw myself backwards, landing with my posterior in the soft dirt and scrabbling backwards even as the massive panel—twice my height and at least that in length—clanged into the courtyard and tilted forward, its full weight slamming into the potential flowerbed where I had been working.

I straightened my right knee and the sole of my boot gonged dully against the lip of the metal, vibrating my leg.

"Pleiti!" I looked up out of my tunnel vision to see Qua Sidram panting up to drop into a crouch by my side. "Are you well?" Qua was head scholar of the Classical philology department, which adjoined the Silvered Library; with the distant precision of shock, I recalled that her office looked out on the courtyard.

"I am, yes," I said, and creaked my way upright, her hand on my elbow though it wasn't entirely necessary. "It didn't hit me." I looked up at the dark spot on the library's wall, the dull inner structure and lines of gas and water pipes dimly visible in the moonlight and the glow of the courtyard lamps. I dropped my gaze again to the flat of metal lying in front of me. "My poor flowers."

Qua scoffed at my concern over the plants. "Absolutely shocking," someone else was saying, and I became aware of more people trickling out of the surrounding buildings and knotting around us.

"—extreme age of some of these buildings—"

"Well, really, maintenance budgets—"

"—never intended to last this long—"

"—put in a request last week, still haven't heard a word—"

"—not sure how I'll get back to work!"

The scatter of conversation dampened with unnatural celerity, and I looked up from brushing the dirt off my trousers to see Ananakuchil Mars striding towards us, with a face like a hailstorm. Ta looked down at the fallen metal. "No one was hurt?"

"No," Qua responded, "although it was a close miss for Pleiti here. Ananakuchil, this cannot be allowed. I told a student to send for maintenance, but I don't know if it's been done . . ."

"Indeed." The chismose crowd had started to fade on Dean Mars's arrival, as scholars, students, and auxiliaries had remembered they had other things to attend to; the remains of it evaporated under ta's gaze. "Send for the Investigators as well," ta said in a quieter tone when only Qua and myself remained within hearing.

Qua frowned. "That façade hasn't been inspected in far too long."

"And it may have been an accident, but let's borrow a

trick from the Speculative faculty, shall we, and consider unlikely scenarios?" Ta turned the glare on me. "Pleiti. Glad you're not injured. I'm sure you want to get cleaned up"—astutely pre-empting my planned excuse—"but do join me in my kantor for a moment on your way out, will you?"

With a resigned nod and a quick, grateful press of Qua's hand, I followed Mars from the courtyard and up the tightly wound space station salvage staircase to ta's kantor.

Mars didn't bother to sit, appraising me sharply instead. "I assume this is something to do with what you and Mossa are after?"

I had half-expected the question, given what ta had said about the Investigators, but I still found it hard to believe. "Do you think so?" Ta's glare intensified. "These buildings are old!" I gestured at the stair we'd ascended and, outside ta's window, the access ramp that was supposed to provide an alternate approach and that had been under construction for at least two years. "They fall apart so frequently, students use it as an excuse when they're late for tutorials!"

"Perhaps," Mars said, deliberate. "But I've never seen a panel fall off the Silvered Library before. Never even seen one wobble."

"You think that was for me?"

"You were the only one in the courtyard, yes?"

"But it was so . . . big."

For the first time in that interview, Mars smiled. "You

don't think you're worth a giant piece of metal? What if it had been aimed at your friend Mossa?"

My mouth went dry with terror. I had no difficulty, it seemed, imagining someone trying to kill Mossa with a chunk of a building. "Believable." I was trying to keep my tone light. "But then—how well did you know her as a student?"

The dean's mouth flattened. "You're trying to pass this off as a joke? I know you two are investigating the murdered Modernist student—"

"And the missing," I said, before I could stop myself.

"Missing?"

"One of the murdered student's friends is also unaccounted for." If Mossa hadn't already informed the university about the number of disappeared she would not thank me for disclosing it.

"I'm sorry to hear that. Well then, it could be that, or someone may be still upset about your very public involvement in the problem with the rector."

I jerked at that; it just seemed so unfair. "You really think—"

"I don't. I don't know. I'm simply urging you to apply some of the protectiveness you clearly hold for your friend to yourself as well."

I found I had nothing to say to that, so I stayed silent. When that didn't work, I nodded.

"Very well." I had already relaxed, was about to turn towards the door, when Mars continued. "Oh, and Pleiti?" Ta's gaze held mine. "I expect to see you in a few hours at the memorial." I had completely forgotten about that; I suspect my chagrin was visible. Ta softened, a bit. "Not going will only worsen the rumors, you know." Ta nodded, releasing me, and I fled as decorously as I could.

Chapter 21

When I arrived back at my rooms, I found Mossa in her usual spot, slumped before the fire in my dressing gown, pondering so deeply that she only murmured indistinctly when I greeted her.

I did not press a conversation. I did not, in any case, feel fit for her style of interrogation at that moment.

Instead, I went past her and drew myself a bath. Finding my own thoughts troublesome, I read while I was soaking, a romp of a novel that had come out during my adolescence, full of the acrobatics and technical ingenuity of well-meaning rail pirates. When I could not stay in the water any longer, I continued reading on my bed. The book let me down in the end, though: when I finished it, I saw it was just the time to start getting ready for the memorial. A few more chapters and I might have missed it. Reluctantly, I dragged myself up and began searching for proper attire.

I emerged, somewhat suitably dressed but in a most unsuitable mood, to find Mossa on her feet and bright-eyed. "Pleiti!" she said, joyously. "When did you come in? I've been waiting for you."

I didn't want to think about the crash of that metal hitting the courtyard, or Mossa not noticing when I arrived. "*Where am I going* is more to the point."

"Indeed!" Mossa said, with every appearance of glee. "Where are we— That is, you have said," she evidenced a sudden switch to caution, "that you prefer to be asked about going on longish, er, long journeys, ideally *before* we depart—"

I eructed a laugh at that, but a weary one. "Yes, ideally before we depart, but also not right now, Mossa, because I need to get to the memorial." I had a sudden strong desire for her to come with me, as though her presence could somehow protect me from the attacks of memory, resentment, and rumor.

"The memorial?" Mossa blinked, taking in my apparel. "I thought you were objecting."

"Oh, I object. But I just saw Dean Mars and ta strongly encouraged me to attend." I tried to appear unconcerned. "It's only a few hours, I suppose it's reasonable." I did not think it reasonable at all.

Mossa straightened. "Where did you see the dean?"

"Oh. I was, as you know, working on the garden, in Soyal? And . . . well, ta's kantor is just there, as you know." I winced as that second *as you know* came out.

"Ta's kantor is on the other side of the building and ta has no reason to pass through the courtyard. Did ta seek you out?" Her gaze had sharpened; she was quivering on the scent; I gave in to the inevitable.

"There was a small accident—well, a largeish accident, really, but no one was hurt—in the courtyard, and so naturally—"

"*What kind of accident?*" Mossa was almost yelling, and did not stop to let me answer, either. "Pleiti, I *told* you to be careful!"

I saved myself from erupting into anger only by remembering how I had felt when Dean Mars suggested I imagine Mossa being attacked that way. Which, incidentally, reminded me that explaining the details was only going to make this worse. "I'm unhurt, Mossa, and I *will* tell you all about it, but—the memorial?"

"Space the memorial!" Mossa said—rudely, but then I quite agreed. "Tell me what happened."

With a sigh, and one last ostentatious glance at my timepiece, I did. I may have minimized somewhat the heft of the falling panel, although I don't think I fooled her. In any case, the data seemed to focus her on practicalities. "What did you do today? Where had you gone before the incident?"

I told her that too, and she blew out in frustration. "Basically everywhere, and antagonizing everyone—no way to narrow it down with that."

"But *really*. It was almost certainly an accident." She didn't bother to answer. "In any case, Mossa, I really must be getting along to this thrice-radiated memorial, so . . ."

"Five minutes," Mossa said, moving towards her room with alacrity. "Ten at most."

"What?" I said, but she was already hidden away, giving me time to temper my relief before she re-emerged, moderately groomed and acceptably dressed.

"There's really no need for you to come," I started feebly, and was amply rewarded when she glowered at me.

"Pleiti! Someone threw half a building at you this evening, I am *not* letting you go to a university event alone! Especially such a dour and unnecessary one," she added under her breath.

"In that case," I said, and smiled as I offered her my arm, savoring the knowledge that possible attacks on me upset her to the point of figurative exaggeration.

Chapter 22

The memorial was held at Pituitary Hall in the Speculative campus, a vast and poorly heated space usually used
for commencements. I suspected, or hoped, that they
had overestimated the attendance, and indeed when we
arrived it was only half-full and, therefore, even chillier
than when complete. Still, I preferred it to most of the
other ceremonial options; there were (at least) thirty-two
egg shapes, decorated with zagging lines or dots, hidden
throughout the jagged-style interior, and though I had
found most of them in the past, the design was intricate
enough that looking for them offered at least some di-
version during the droning lies about the rector and his
supposed accomplishments. Most people wore brown, to
represent Earth, or the undyed fabrics typical of the early
settlement, and when I turned my gaze to the collective,

I was reminded of an image I had read of many times in Classical literature but only seen for myself during our long drive on Io: snow on soil.

I was embarrassingly pleased that Mossa was with me; her presence by my side, emitting the faintest of snorts at the most egregious flourishes of hagiography, was a balm. I had briefly, on the walk over, fallen in thrall of the idea that this must be love: for her to so willingly join in this awful business only to be a succor (and in her mind probably protection) to me. It wasn't until the ceremony was well under way that I recognized that it was no kind of sacrifice to her: immune to the undercurrents of guilt, resentment, and injustice that so perturbed me, she was observing the social rite with a bass note of fascination.

At long last, the erai of the university felt they had given enough reverence to a dead comemierda who had in his selfishness threatened their entire academic project, and left off. The by then unaccustomed silence was quickly populated by a rumble of movement, a murmur of quiet voices commenting and critiquing, extrapolating and snarking. It sounded almost like a natural phenomenon, I thought idly as Mossa and I stood; like the overlapping coos of pigeons or the rising, falling cadence of crickets, as though I could perceive (I was clearly overexhausted) some kind of communal consciousness or at least directionality—

I stiffened. I could, though. I could. The direction of a solid plurality of the murmurs was *at me.*

I remembered with sudden clarity what Dean Mars had said: *Not going will only worsen the rumors.* I had not thought much of it at the time; my objection to the memorial had been entirely due to my feelings of ethical dissonance, not to say hypocrisy, on the part of the university and the community in general. I had not realized (though I should have) that I would, myself, be so public the object of curiosity, conjecture, and questions, and only now did I understand that while not going might have made it worse, going had made it far more painful.

"Mossa!" I whispered urgently.

"Hmm?" She appeared to be observing the interaction between several members of the Speculative faculty's administrative arm; I was too panicked to notice more.

"Can we leave now? Right now, quickly, Mossa?"

"What, now?" She looked round at me, clocked my terror, and scanned the room, a short triangular knife appearing in her hand. "Who—"

"Mossa!" I hissed, social anguish forgotten for the moment. "Why are you carrying that?"

"The whip-lasso is conspicuous in this sort of clothing. Who did you—"

A don from the Speculative faculty that I knew only by sight had arrived within hailing distance. "Pleiti, isn't it?" He managed to make his tone sound cultivated even while modulating it to the volume necessary to hit its target at ten paces. "I wondered if I might have a moment to ask"—his voice dropped rapidly as he came closer, so that by this point it was positively intimate—"about the last moments of the rector. On *this* planet, at least." A deprecating chuckle.

"Oh, I see." Mossa disappeared her knife and flashed

her insignia. "Official business. Very immediate." She tugged on my arm and, offering what I hoped looked like a helpless smile over my shoulder, I followed her out the side exit.

- - - - - - - -

Chapter 23

Mossa hurried me away from the hall at speed. Initially I was too gratified to be out of there to think much on our route, but when she drew me down Weilo instead of continuing on Blinkstart towards my rooms I stopped, or tried to.

"Come on!" Mossa said, looking back at me.

"But—where are we going?"

"To the station."

I gaped at her. A wave of schoolchildren in matching celadon-tinted atmoscarfs, proceeding in the opposite direction, broke around us with curious looks and not a few giggles. It was a little past dawn, the streetlights already dimming and the shops variously opening or recently closed, depending on their schedules. Mossa *had* mentioned something about a journey, I remembered.

"Well then," I said, recovering or attempting to, "where are we going?"

For the sly smile she flashed me—just a half smile really, a quarter, one edge of her lips curling up—I would have followed her anywhere. "I'll tell you along the way. Once we have some privacy," she added over her shoulder as we set off again, perhaps to make it clear we would not be discussing it in the street.

"I suppose you've packed a bag for me?" I asked, resigned.

The expression she sent back towards me was at least seven-eighths of a grin. "I did indeed, but I'll have to send someone to the porter's lodge for it, I wasn't going to carry our valises to *that* shambles."

I laughed with her and the morning felt fresh despite my exhaustion, Valdegeld's antique streets sparkling with possibilities: festivals, cream teas, friendship, etching exhibits, opera, the solutions to all mysteries, and true love. The elation of escaping the memorial service, doubtless, but I enjoyed it all the same.

I scanned the boards automatically when we entered the station, looking for a clue as to where we might be going, but after entrusting one of the station porters to bring our equipage, Mossa led me down an unobtrusive passage by the waiting room, and we found ourselves on an isolated, short andén facing a small spur off the ring, where a railcar of only two wagons awaited.

"Investigators' private railcar," Mossa explained, as we boarded. "I called for it yesterday, thinking we might need it. We have a long journey ahead of us, and we will want quiet and solitude I think."

"And the second wagon?" I had noticed the bars on its windows.

"It's possible we will be bringing someone back with us."

"You found a clue, then?" I thought, with only a little chagrin, of all my fruitless searches earlier that day.

"I did, I did. I was going to tell you before we set out," Mossa said, looking rueful, "but, as you know, events overcame us." She hesitated. "It's well past bedtime, and we're both quite tired, you in particular have had an exhausting day—"

"Come now, Mossa!"

"—what with," she went on inexorably, "the rather unsubtle murder attempts—"

"Mossa!"

"Oh, if you insist. We have to wait for our luggage in any case. I'll give you the basics and then if you think of them as you repose, we can compare conclusions in a few hours."

"Good enough."

"Well." Her eyes gleamed with the chase. "I've been to the Investigators' bureau here. Ah, that reminds me." She reached into her pocket and tossed a package on the ledge table below the windows. "Sakura-mochi."

I pounced. There was a single agricultural platform that fabricated the treats using ingredients from their small sakura orchard and minuscule rice paddy, but the only sweetshop that traded with them was on the other side of Valdegeld and it was rare that I happened to pass when they happened to have a stock. I wouldn't have expected Mossa to remember my fondness for that flavor, the fresh stridency of the leaf folded around the gentle aroma of the mochi.

"I have another missing person to add to our constellation," Mossa went on, watching my reaction to the box of mochi with amusement. "There's a reason we didn't notice this one before: she was listed not as a missing person, but as a fugitive." She passed me a laminate, and I temporarily abandoned the sweets in its favor.

"Another one from the Speculative faculty."

"Not quite a pattern," Mossa agreed, "but disproportionate to their representation in the university as a whole. And look at this." Mossa leaned over to tap the dossier, and I was briefly distracted by the rounding of her forearm, the neatness of her pointing finger, the skin with its warmth and its myriad minuscule creases. "Jolifan Lup, a Speculative engineer, was accused of stealing funds—a rather complex process of embezzlement—*and* also plans for an experimental atmoshield."

I considered the implications. Atmoshields were large investments, but the number of platforms was increasing; a new version that was preferable in some way would be worth quite a lot. And—had she stolen the funds from the Speculative bursary? If so, that would be a link with Elemaya.

As I opened my mouth to ask, however, there was the ding of the door alert: our bags had arrived. Once everything was loaded, Mossa checked the schedule to confirm that there was enough of a gap in the regular railcars for safety, and then we pulled out to the ring turning.

"East or west, Pleiti?" she asked, cheerfully.

I raised my eyebrows, but decided not to take the bait. I would work out the reason for her cavalier attitude towards navigation later, silently, preferably while Mossa was asleep and with the railcar timetable to hand. "East," I said decisively. Mossa nodded approvingly, turned the crank to engage the correct curve, and we glided off.

Chapter 24

The first part of our journey took us through some of the most thickly platform'd stretches of Giant's ring network. Our private railcar could bypass without stopping, but the frequency of well-appointed stations flashing by our windows was distracting, and Mossa needed to keep referring to the official timetable to be sure that we would not overtake a scheduled wagon. Thrice we pulled off into station sidings to allow other railcars to pass or accrue more distance.

In addition to the bag which Mossa had so thoughtfully packed without my knowledge, there were two large hampers bearing the unmistakable sigil of Supal Provisioners. I was a little surprised, then, when Mossa ducked out while we were adjusting our timings at the Yaste station and returned with four large packets of food, still warm in their wrappers. I looked from them to the hamper. "A particular favorite? Or is this going to be a very long journey indeed?"

Mossa favored me with a full smile. I had noticed she seemed more relaxed on railcar rides, at least when we were alone. "Both, really. The sautéed cabbage and protein from Té食 is excellent, but then so are the rolled pupusas from San Guívin's. I rarely pass through Yaste without taking advantage of the opportunity to enjoy one or both. And it will, indeed, be a very long journey."

"That long? What am I to do about my tutorials?"

"I would suggest a wire to Dean Mars now. But we are nearly to half-term holidays, you won't miss so very much. I hope."

Grumpily, I disembarked to take her advice. The pupusas went a long way to cheering me, however. And perhaps some extra holiday would be wise; I certainly hadn't been distinguishing myself in my work ethic recently.

After Yaste the platforms were somewhat less frequent, as were the railcars between them, and we traveled faster. I took some time to familiarize myself with the manifold comforts offered by a private railcar, though at that stage just the idea of being alone in that small compartment with Mossa, at no risk of anyone entering to interrupt us, nor of walls falling, nor of dons with intrusive questions, was luxury enough. So luxurious, in fact, that I had trouble keeping my eyes open, and may have dozed.

Mossa touched my shoulder. "I've unfolded one of the beds, Pleiti. You may as well rest comfortably." I was at that point too tired to argue.

When I woke, it was to see Mossa awake, staring out the window at the fog. I rose, sidled into the tiny washroom—there was a slightly larger cabinet for actual showers, although I wasn't sure my need would extend to the point of using it—and splashed water on my face. When I returned, Mossa had curled up on the bed and was already snoring softly. It would be some time before I heard more about her theory, and our destination.

Poking about in my valise I discovered that Mossa had packed several tomes for me, both work and leisure, and with her usual keenness had selected texts that I would have chosen myself. I picked out one that had been waiting some months for my attention, a treatise on commonly believed myths about the late Classical age that had been proved untrue. But as often as not I left it lying in my lap while I stared out the window. Or, as often (let me admit it), observed Mossa as she slept. I plumbed the fractals of my desires: the physical urge, so like an addiction; but also the pervasive, contradictory drives for proximity and independence informing all of our dance around commuting or cohabitation, collaborating or compartmentalizing. What *did* I want? After several hours, considerable efforts of cognition, and an ignominious delve into the hamper for snacks, I had arrived only at the unoriginal conclusion that lust was irrational, an unrepeatable experiment, and love inexplicable.

Which implied, I continued glumly, munching on some emping, that all of our academic striving and posturing was meaningless. Either love—and its corollary hate, I thought, remembering the vicious slash that had ended Strevan's life—could overturn all our sweats of logic and theory in an instant or—and?—we were studying the wrong thing.

I was at this dismal stage, beginning to wonder what a Department of Attachment and Affection Studies would look like in the Classical, Modern, and Speculative faculties, when Mossa opened her eyes and sat up. And smiled.

My mood soared immediately, and explaining why no longer seemed so important. "Sleep well?"

"Tolerably." She yawned, stretching. It occurred to me that Mossa's investigatory approach, which was based in large part on character portraits and narrative relationships, might be considered to include theories of love and hate. "Where are we?"

"Ah . . ." I glanced at the relevant panel. "We passed Estrocs some while ago." Only one of the bulbs representing stations to come remained lit. "I take it we're not going to Prathyns?"

"No, no indeed." Mossa scrubbed at her face with her palms. "I must tell you, Pleiti, this is no more than an idea, a most tenuous whim—but—" (in answer to my non-verbal sound expressing skepticism at her hesitancy, considering how often she was correct)—"very well, let me use the washroom and I'll tell you my theory."

I had thought that perhaps we were circumnavigating the planet, traversing the vast unsettled arc of Giant in order to come upon our quarry from an unexpected direction, although it certainly seemed a time-consuming means of achieving surprise. And, indeed, Mossa's reasoning was quite different.

"I believe," she said; then added, still hesitant, "that is, I speculate—based, Pleiti, in large part on your acute observation about the composition of the missing group—I think that they have settled an unauthorized platform, somewhere out here in the 'empty seven-eighths.'"

That was startling to the point of incredulity, seemed entirely unlikely if not impossible—*how* could they manage that and *why* on Giant would they want to try and *how* could they stay hidden and—but I had held so much worry over those missing people, deepening like a panicked heartbeat since I found Strevan's corpse, and what came out was a gust of relief: "Then you think they're safe? All those missing people? The students?"

Mossa was looking at me with an intensity I couldn't interpret. She seemed almost hesitant to speak. "As I said, it is mere supposition." I gave her another pointed look, and she hemmed slightly. "In Chaac, when we spoke to Elemaya's family, you were . . . concerned about the issue of false hope."

"Ah. Yes, with family, but—" I waved it aside. "Call it a theory, but still: You think they are well?"

"*Well* in the sense that they have not been murdered like Strevan, I *believe* so. Whether living in such circumstances, and making the dubious choice to do so, can be considered completely *well* . . ."

"Yes, why would they be living out here?" I turned to peer out the window, as though it would show me anything but fitfully torquing gases.

"I believe they are attempting self-sufficiency."

I tried to assimilate that into my still reverberating

worldview. "Why?" I asked at last, but Mossa remained silent as I continued to work through it. "You think all these isolated people went off someplace where they'd be even more isolated? Oh! The stolen atmoshield plans?"

"That was a crucial hint to their purpose, once I connected the thief to the disappeared."

"How will we find them out here, anyway? There are thousands upon thousands of kilometers of ring to search!" *I might as well quit my job,* I thought, in a tone of internal irony, and was surprised at how plausible that idea seemed.

"I do have a suspicion, related to that insight about their isolation, in fact." I waited. Part of the trick with Mossa, I had found, was waiting longer than I expected to. It really wasn't so very long, once I had recalibrated. "My guess is we are going to the antipode of Valdegeld." Mossa proposed that they would almost certainly choose an intersection of rings, as opposed to a single-ring platform. "The timing of the disappearances suggests that this group has every intention of expanding, and indeed I believe all founders of utopias believe that their settlements will prosper and attract more inhabitants."

"Utopia?"

She waved her hand. "Or autonomy, if you prefer, or safety from persecution. Heroism, perhaps." I gaped, and she quirked an eyebrow, then went on. "Whether it is ills or aspirations, they will believe that what drives them affects many others, who will willingly join, thereby demonstrating the correctness of the philosophy."

"And if those ills, or the opposition to their aspirations, is identified with Valdegeld . . ."

"Then," Mossa agreed, "the point directly opposite to Valdegeld would carry symbolic weight."

A long way to go for a theory based on antagonism and wounded pride, I thought, leaning back to contemplate it. And again, they weren't doing anyone any harm out here—

Mossa, no doubt having concluded that I had reached that point in my cogitations, spoke again. "I do have another qualm about their safety. They may well be sharing this remote, isolated platform with a murderer."

We had ample time, over the next days of travel along lonely, mist-shrouded swaths of ring, to debate Mossa's reasoning and prioritize a list of possible alternative locations. Ample time, even, in between long stretches of sitting in silence, watching the colors of the mist swirling by, for our talk to turn to other, less comfortable questions.

"Why did the memorial upset you so much?"

I turned to Mossa, incredulous, and she waved her hand. "I understand, people were going to pester you. But you are not a person who is so very dependent on other people's opinion." She hesitated; I was busy digesting that appraisal of my character. "You do care considerably about your responsibilities; your, your, position . . ."

I sighed, forcing myself to think about the question. "I do, and I will admit, I resented that the university expected me to go, as if it were part of my job. But mainly, I simply did not want to think about the rector, and what he did.

I *especially* did not want to hear other people praising or excusing him, but in all honesty I wanted to avoid thinking about his actions at all myself."

Mossa nodded. "It's because the rector ruined your chances." My face must have shown my confusion. "Your chances to achieve your purpose as a Classical scholar, to ascertain a potential ecosystem and put it into practice. The chances of returning to Earth." I noticed she didn't say *your* that time, as was appropriate, since that chance belonged, or should have, to all of us.

"No, that's not it." I hadn't known myself until she articulated that and it clanged wrong. "It's—" I struggled, but it was so unusual for Mossa not to understand something, it seemed important to clarify it. "I never really felt it was possible. I mean, reading about Earth, it was like . . . reading about Oz, or Pern, or Quistable. You want it to be your reality so much, but you also know it isn't real. I believed in what I was doing, rationally I thought—think—it can happen, but it always felt . . . insubstantial somehow."

Mossa stroked my wrist. "The rector made it real."

"It almost, almost feels possible." I took a breath, realized I was gasping. "And . . . it was easier when it was impossible, as opposed to . . . to . . ."

She waited.

"What hurts," I continued painfully, "is that maybe it would have been possible, if a few human beings hadn't fucked it up."

"Ah," said Mossa, and we resolved into silence again.

Chapter 25

Both of the seats in the wagon unfolded into beds—and there were another two in the other wagon—but they were too narrow for two to share and in any case Mossa had decreed that we sleep in turns, a precaution with which I readily agreed once I had imagined the possibility of approaching an unknown, unmapped, ungoverned platform as we both slept.

When I imagined it like that, however, the very concept seemed impossible. A platform that no one knew about?

"Why not?" Mossa asked me, eyebrow quirked. "Do we know so much about what happens on Giant?"

I frowned. Earth had been almost obsessively mapped, settled, surveilled, examined, and analyzed. Its inhabitants—our ancestors—had felt, towards the end of their tenure there, that the possibilities for terrestrial exploration were exhausted, although they evidently did not know enough to prevent its deterioration into unlivability.

Giant, on the other hand, was far less documented. To someone like me, largely uninterested in the Modern sciences, that seemed quite reasonable; after all, there was little other than our constructions that stayed constant long enough to be mapped, little that could be documented. Gases, moons, but no organisms (that we had yet found) bigger than microbes (and there was an ongoing debate in the interstices of the Classical and Modern faculties as to whether those microbes were native or had been brought with us). It was easy to assume that, beyond the details of the endlessly changing and ephemeral swirls of gas, the vast surface of the planet was essentially uniform, and its depths a mystery without meaning.

We did not have satellites scanning Giant's orb; such capacity in those areas as still existed was largely orbiting Earth, hoping for clues about the evolution of its apocalypse. I supposed, vaguely, that rings were periodically checked all along their circumference for maintenance reasons, but I had no idea how often that happened. Giant was simply too large to circumnavigate lightly.

It was so large that figuring out where we were was a challenge. I supposed that Mossa had some means of calculating how far we'd traveled, since the railcar surely measured its own speed. Once we'd left the last station behind (I assumed), such speed should be fairly constant, making the maths relatively simple. However, when I mentioned this Mossa pointed out how much the varying winds could affect our speed.

"The calculations could be done," she agreed, "indeed, the railcar measures distance traveled as a matter of course. But it's somewhat inexact. Typically there's a corrective applied at every platform, but out here that's not possible."

As an additional measure, she had packed the portable qibla astrolabe I kept in my rooms, a gift from my parents when I left our platform to which I assigned mostly sentimental value, since I did not travel enough (or, to be honest, indulge in physical prayer often enough) to make much use of it. (Indeed, I had not consulted it once during our stay on Io, though Mossa had considerately packed it for me on that occasion as well.) It was thanks to that rather outdated device that we were aware when we approached the point opposite Valdegeld, and thus were both awake and at least somewhat alert when we came suddenly upon a platform where no platform should be.

The first I saw of it was green, unexpected as a slap after the days of ochre and russet and pallid yellow fog. Of course they would need their own crops. Mossa slowed the railcar, letting us observe the cultivations—beans, I saw, and what might be squash—but she didn't stop it until we reached a cluster of small edifices. And, I saw as we trailed into immobility, people, more of them emerging as we arrived.

The unnoticed hum of our railcar stopped for the first time in days.

"Incredible," I murmured, watching the arriving figures from the window. Mossa cast me a sardonic glance. "They're just so far from everything!" I said, a bit defensively. It was true that any platform, no matter how close to its neighbor, was surrounded by dense fog, freezing temperatures, and the absence of anything to stand on, and might feel just as isolated. But the people living here were truly far from anyone else, farther than it had been physically possible to be while living on Earth. "No trade. No emergency support. What if something happens?"

"I can only assume that this is what they want. Some of them, at least. Come along, Pleiti, you can practice ethnography later. We have a murder to solve."

Chapter 26

Mossa caused the door to slide, and a breath of fresh air came in, surprisingly warm. We exchanged glances: the stolen plans for the new atmoshield model had promised better heat retention. Mossa swung herself out of the car and I went to follow.

There was no station, no andén, leaving a moderate drop and a slight gap between the railcar and the platform. It was far too narrow for me to fall through, but wide enough to see the thicker gases below us, and I had to steel myself to take the long step over and down. I glanced along the ring ahead of us; no andén anywhere, although I did see a railcar, a single wagon, stopped toward the far end of the platform. Then I looked around at the grouping of strangers with familiar faces: the missing.

I was conscious of another layer of relief: for all my assurances to Mossa of my confidence in her theories, I evidently had not completely believed the missing were safe
(safe relative to Strevan, in any case). Most of the faces
around us were easily recognizable from the dossiers of
missing people, and each added to my satisfaction; I also
noted others that I was positive had not been among the
group we knew about. It was odd to see the faces from
those laminates I had pored over watching me; some with
longer hair, some looking a bit tireder or thinner. I recognized Mippala Noo, one of the kitchen workers from
Valdegeld, and noticed that he was standing close with
someone whose face I didn't know. Had they brought rel-
atives, friends, lovers from other platforms—more missing that we hadn't known about?

I could feel Mossa, who as I have mentioned felt little
compunction to fill silences, nonetheless gearing herself
to talk, when one of our observers spoke first.

"Who are you?" she demanded. I hadn't recognized her
at first, but I now realized it was Jolifan Lup, the engineer
who had been accused of theft and embezzlement. Her
likeness in the dossier Mossa had shown me on the railcar
was perhaps four or five years old, and she was changed
enough that I suspected at least some of those years had
been spent in harsh conditions. I thought about how this
independent platform must have been constructed, how
the people on it might have survived until the first crops,
what it must be like to live there even now, and smothered
a shudder.

She spoke again, without noticeable softening. "Do you need help?"

Help? This was so surprising to me that I was still off-balance when Mossa said: "Not the kind of help you mean. We did, however, come here to ask for your assistance in apprehending a murderer."

A muttering rose among the crowd surrounding us, but it was perhaps more puzzled than aggressive, and then a young woman—Zebaia Elemaya—edged forward. "It's Strevan, isn't it? He's dead?"

There was no pub or restaurant or inn, as such, on the platform, but we were able to repair to one of the residences for some privacy. I expected little more than a shack, and indeed it was clear that materials were scarce, but the design was exceedingly clever and the construction well engineered. A fire gulped gas merrily in the hearth, but the furniture was rudimentary and uncushioned. Lup, who seemed to be the leader, or at least the loudest, wanted to join us; Mossa insisted on privacy, but I was sure she was waiting just outside, probably listening to everything she could catch.

"Why did you conclude that Strevan's is the murder we are investigating?" Mossa queried softly while I let my eye wander over the interior.

Elemaya was sitting in an angle of the wall, either because she thought it right to give up her chairs to the visitors or because she already knew that to be the most comfortable spot. Her eyes were on her hands and her hands in her lap, and though she could only be a decade or so younger than I, she looked almost like a child.

"He was supposed to come," she said. "That is . . . I thought I had convinced him. He was supposed to come on the next railcar run. It was not certain, but . . . I thought if he didn't come, he would at least send a message, or . . . when he didn't, I started to think something had happened."

"When you met at the Cat Club, you were persuading him to join you here?"

"I was trying." There was a long pause. "We'd been talking about it for some time. He . . . he went back and forth: sometimes all he wanted was to get away from Valdegeld and everything he hated about it; sometimes he thought he could show them his worth best by staying."

I wondered whether the things Strevan had hated about Valdegeld were the same things I loved about it.

Elemaya sighed, still looking at her hands. "He loved that stupid club, loved that he belonged to it, loved the luxury of it. He pretended that he only took me there because it was convenient or there was some special dish he liked, but really it was because he liked being able to invite someone." She looked up at Mossa. "But there was a part of him that wanted to be better than that! I know there was. He loved the old stories of settlement, all the sacrifices and hardships, and I explained to him how we finally had a chance to prove ourselves out here, how we could show that we were as willing and capable as the settlers, and like them, we could build something for the future."

Out of her line of sight, I let myself grimace: I knew how Mossa felt about equating *more ascetic* with *better.*

Mossa, naturally, showed none of that, instead leaning forward slightly in the attitude of a perfect listener, if not a disciple. "Tell me about what you're building here."

Elemaya spoke with intensity and single-mindedness about the need for a place outside the restrictive oversight of the organizing committees of Giant, away from the grasping universities; about the importance of innovation, and how the ideas of the young were being stifled or appropriated; about freedom and expansion and, again, about proving themselves, showing that they could survive independently.

I lingered by the wall, trying not to let my attention drift too far from her fanaticism, which retrod the same ground in slightly different fashion many times over. When I could concentrate no more, I observed the building we were in, which interested me far more. There was an apparently open seam which, when I inspected it, turned out to be sealed with some form of atmoshield, an interesting solution for ventilation and temperature modulation.

"I am willing to consider the possibility that you did not murder your conlunarian." Judging by the adamantine tones, Mossa felt she had exhausted the benefits of playing the sympathetic ear; from Elemaya's widened eyes, she hadn't missed the change. "We still need to find out who did. The deed occurred," she continued over Elemaya's anxious babbled defense, "not too long after your meal with Strevan at the Cat Club. The more you can tell us about that—what occurred, his mien, his statements, where he was going when you parted—*anything* may be fundamental in bringing his murderer to justice."

"And you're certain it was murder?" Elemaya faltered. "Not simply some . . . some accident?"

"Very certain," I said from my corner, allowing the horrid memory to lend conviction to my voice.

I learned far more than I wanted to know about a meal at the Cat Club: the service, the menu, the ambient animations, the pervasive felines. Frightened or defensive, Elemaya related all in great detail.

"And then?" Mossa asked.

"He walked me out, a few blocks. I was about to leave, you see, to come here, and so . . . I wanted to take every opportunity to convince him."

"And he was not convinced?"

"He said he'd think about it. I reminded him about the timing for the next run, about the . . . the procedure."

Mossa ignored the obvious shiftiness there. "And then?"

"Then what? I didn't see him again." She sounded not distraught so much as sad, as though only then realizing that she never would.

"Then where did you go?"

"I came here."

"Directly?"

"As directly as I could. We, er . . ." She looked at the door.

Mossa raised her voice and enunciated. "May I remind you that we are conducting an investigation into the murder of your friend. I am not here to deal with the legality, or not, of this installation, and if I were it would be too late in any case. It is abundantly clear that you have found some irregular and probably perilous means of access to a railcar of some description. My concern at the moment—and that's not to say it won't change, operating a railcar without sufficient coordination is dangerous for others as well as for yourselves—my concern *at the moment* is whether or not you were in a position to murder Strevan. How did you come here after leaving him?"

After one more glance at the door, and presumably reassured when Lup didn't barge through it to stop her, Elemaya lowered her eyes to her hands again. "We have to be very careful with the schedules, of course, especially at such crowded places as Valdegeld. I took a railcar to Cynkar, and there—you know they have a bridge that spans the 1'02°? I had arranged to meet our railcar there. It's one wagon, you know, so when there's a long enough gap it can stop under the bridge, and then we just swing down to it."

I closed my eyes in a futile effort not to imagine that.

"I suppose your arrival here would then limit when you could have left Valdegeld . . ." When I looked again Mossa was frowning; I could guess she was somewhat dubious about the value of the witnesses here in terms of timing, although I was also fairly sure she had discounted Elemaya as a suspect. "Did you by any chance speak with anyone in Cynkar?"

Elemaya shrugged. "I bought some food packets. It's a long ride."

Mossa's expression remained severe. "Do you have any idea who might have wanted to kill Strevan?"

Elemaya shook her head.

"Could he have been killed because he knew about this place?"

Mossa's tone had gone gentle again, and indeed Elemaya's expression was newly horrified. "No! Surely not! He didn't—well, I suppose he knew some things about this place, Potivance—" one of the Speculative scholars who had disappeared, I remembered—"had been telling us about it for months, and Jolifan when she came back for, ah, supplies. But he wasn't proselytizing it—*I* was the one that was trying to convince people to come. He hadn't even decided!"

Mossa made a non-committal sound.

"I'm sure he annoyed lots of people. He was . . . ambitious. But then, everyone at Valdegeld is, aren't they, or they wouldn't be there? But most of them smooth it over in that certain way that means it's all right, and Strevan didn't know how to do that. He would talk about being a don someday, and not realize," Elemaya sniffed, tears welling up for the first time in our interview, "how, how very unlikely that was. He just didn't . . . it wasn't that he wanted to do research all the time, he just wanted to show them, d'you know?" Her Ionian accent was becoming more pronounced as well. "So, yes, I can imagine people being angry at him. He would not get something he wanted, and then say it was all stacked against him and rage about it and . . . I *told* him, I told him they would never give him what he wanted, never forget that he was from Io. But I didn't think they would *kill* him." She had to gulp air again. "I knew he should have come here."

Chapter 27

"Before we go," Mossa stood and stretched, "could I have a look at your railcar?"

Elemaya hesitated, sensing a trap or perhaps simply unsure if her authority extended so far, but Mossa was already out the door. I followed her closely enough to see Lup, who must have been waiting just outside, start talking with her. Lup's soliloquy—for I didn't see Mossa utter a word—was earnest and heavy with gesticulation. I caught the phrase "Little Earth," and had to look away quickly so as not to lose my composure. Elemaya was beside me, no longer weeping but red-eyed and biting her lip, and I leaned toward her. "Your brothers are concerned about you."

I had thought she might get defensive, but she smiled, and fondly. "I'll send for them as soon as things are a bit better here." I glanced around the rather stark platform, wondering just how bad it was. Could they have enough to eat, really? How much were they bringing in from outside? Did they have a medic?

"They'll be allowed to come?" I asked.

"Oh, they can't come directly here anyway. I'll come up with some excuse and meet them, then bring them along." Her face sombered. "Not in Valdegeld, probably. But they'll like it here."

I looked again at the bare platform, empty of amenities, sparse of society, precarious in every way, and wondered again at our human tendency to romanticize the imposition of unnecessary obstacles into our lives.

Ahead of us, Mossa was deploying her excellent skills at ignoring people, allowing Lup to stroll alongside so immersed in a one-sided conversation that she did not even realize where she was going until they were beside the railcar. It was a slightly older model, subtle details of its window borders and paneling and palette all suggesting that it had been new some decade and a half earlier. Still, it was not so old, nor so decrepit, as to be likely abandoned. A theft? Or, more interestingly, a donation?

I could not make out any identifying markings, but Mossa turned away from it with an abruptness that told me she had found what she was looking for, and I certainly did not wish to linger any longer, so I followed her with alacrity to our own wagons.

We had attracted a small following, which I took to be the entire population of the platform or nearly, and when we had reached our railcar Mossa turned to address them. "No one here wishes to return? Everyone is here of free will?"

"Of course they are!" Lup bridled, but Mossa waited, looking from face to face.

"If anyone wishes to return," she persisted, "we can take you immediately. You need fear no repercussions, neither from the organizational committees in Yaste nor from those here."

"Of course there wouldn't be repercussions," Elemaya said, apparently emboldened by her familiarity with us. "Everyone is here because they wanted to come."

"That doesn't mean they want to stay," Mossa responded, but gently, and though she cast her gaze around the circled figures again, none made any gesture or indication of wanting to join us. Turning, she climbed into the railcar. I followed, full of relief, although I did not feel entirely comfortable until the door had closed and we had started back the way we came; not, in fact, until all we could see out the windows was the dense fog of the planet and we were once again cocooned in aloneness.

At that point I let out an enormous sigh.

"Was it really so bad, Pleiti?" Mossa asked mildly.

"Must have been," I retorted, "seeing as you've already put the tea on." She had swept the button for hot water as soon as we were out of sight of the platform.

Mossa laughed. "All right, then, fairly grim. Shall we have a real go at that second hamper? Fanatics make me hungry."

I should have been dreading the days of travel ahead of us, eerie with solitude and the swaying of storms, but in that moment of camaraderie and ease I was rather wishing the ride would be even longer.

The remaining hamper offered cheese, fruits, various shapes and thicknesses of hard biscuits flecked with various herbs, krupuk and emping, rabbit jerky, duck paté, walnut and fruit churchkhela, jars of chutneys and jams, piquant gram vadei, sesame halva, and four small flasks of, I discovered with surprise and approval when I sniffed, mezcal.

After sampling the provisions, and consuming a full pot of tea with a splash or two of mezcal in the later cups, I felt warm and comfortable. It was dark out, and I should have been sleepy, but I could not help picking at the memory of the strange place we had just been, their defiance and silliness and courage.

"What do you think will happen to them?"

"Oh, they'll be found, eventually." Mossa plucked another kumquat lazily. "A maintenance run, a shuttle passing over where someone looks down at the wrong moment. A scientific expedition, perhaps. Possibly someone will give them up, either one of the members who tires of the austere and lonely life or one of their suppliers."

"I had thought," I said hesitatingly, "that I might find a way to get them some produce from my family's platform, or at least some satellite mirror time, but—" I grimaced at my foolishness, and drank.

"No," Mossa said, agreeing with my unspoken conclusion. "Too easily traced, any of it, if someone decides to look. And, naturally, there are the chances of someone circumnavigating the planet on a whim, or someone on one of the moons catching a glimpse with a telescope, or simply the expansion of the platform network."

"And then?" I asked, copying the Ionian intonation Mossa had used to encourage Elemaya.

She flashed me a half smile. "It depends how long before they are found, and their attitudes. If they have time to get well-established *and* to work their way out of this determination to prove their independence, their resourcefulness, their—" a mueca that could have been despair over their quixocity or anger at the context that elicited it—"their *self-worth,* if they can get past all that, well, perhaps they may be able to set up some kind of relationship, trade . . . But truly, the organizing committees will not like the idea of a platform that doesn't answer to them."

"And with some reason," I pointed out. "It could become a haven for criminals—"

Mossa angled an extremely skeptical look. "Your telenovelas again?"

"Well then, for people who wish to disappear, as these did, for better or worse reasons! Think of all the time you spent tracking them. And our situation here is still precarious enough to be worried about ungoverned actions that affect our life support, threaten the integrity of the rings . . ."

"Indeed," Mossa retorted, "and such actions could just as easily come from within the network supposedly governed by the organizing committee, from the university, perhaps?" She raised her eyebrows at me until I nodded reluctant agreement.

"Spandal."

"Indeed." Mossa raised her cup. "And not only him, to be sure. I didn't want to bring it up, because they were already insupportable, but consider how Lup might describe the situation with the atmoshield?"

That had already occurred to even my academiphiliac mind. "No doubt," I said with a sigh, "it was the university that stole her invention, and the money was only her due."

"I don't know that she's wrong, and to be honest, I can't be fucked to find out." Mossa took another sip, and I wondered if she was a little flown already. "Another reason why I didn't bring it up: I'd rather not feel obligated to investigate. Although perhaps I will yet." She sighed, and reached out in a desultory way for another vadei to nibble on. "For the moment, however, as far as we know this group is *not* harboring criminals or offering any threat to anyone besides themselves, and the organizing committees are unlikely to look at the situation dispassionately. In fact, between these people trying to prove their capacity for independence and the committees trying to affirm the impossibility of living independently—" She made an impatient gesture.

There was a silence.

"So we proceed delicately, then," I offered cautiously, and was rewarded by a quarter smile.

"Indeed. The further I can stay from this problem the happier I'll be." She yawned, then croqued the last of the vadei and took another. Watching her eat was making me hungry again, and I took a beautifully rubescent church-khela from the basket. There was a contented pause.

"Did Lup really call the place 'Little Earth'?" I asked at last.

Mossa laughed. "She did. In all seriousness."

"Is it after *Earth* Earth, or that disastrous Mars settlement, or— Never mind, I don't want to know."

"Good," replied Mossa, still amused, "because she didn't say, and our task is a different one. Now, Pleiti, we have found the missing; the question remains: can we find the murderer?"

Chapter 28

I refilled my cup and nursed its heat in my hands, considering what clues we had. Was the remote settlement we had just left intrinsic or a mere distraction? Had Strevan been killed for being brash, annoying, out of step with Valdegeld, or had he done something more serious? I raised my eyes to the blank wall and felt a flick of irritation: Why hadn't Mossa yet laid out her usual storyboard, organizing the strands of the investigation into— Wait.

I looked at Mossa: she was studying the toe of her slipper. Fury rose in me as strong and sudden as desire. "You already know who did it!"

She looked up, immediately apologetic. "I—I do suspect so, Pleiti, but—" I growled. "All right, yes, I am . . . not certain, but, erm, confident. But Pleiti, I promise, this was not meant as a test or a tease!" She hesitated, then flurried on. "You might remember we once talked about how, how we both enjoy the parts of our jobs carried out in solitary contemplation?" I nodded, remembering: the exotic scent of woodsmoke, the enticing suggestion of connection. "Well . . ." Mossa hemmed. "I have realized, over the past few months that, while solitude is far preferable to most people, discussing case narratives with you is both more pleasant and more useful and . . . well, in short, I would rather do that."

I was overwhelmed for an uncounted space of time; then I marshaled my intellect (*was it my intellect that attracted her?*) and set to it. "I do appreciate that, Mossa, and you know I am happy to work with you, but I promise you, I have at this time no coherent narrative for the case, so I strongly suggest that you present yours and I will tell you if I can find any inconsistencies."

"Quite right, Pleiti," she said so humbly that I almost forgave her when she pulled out a set of storyboard cards already prepared and began affixing them to the wall, much as if she had planned that entire sequence. "Well then! Let us take as an initial premise—which we may later disprove or change—that the murder had something to do with the libertopian settlement LARP we just left."

"Mossa! I thought you wanted them to survive!" I protested, startled into laughter by her sudden harshness.

She cut her hand sideways, a truncated motion of dismissal. "I think they're self-indulgent and foolish— although I will admit," grudgingly, "that they are managing better than I would have expected. But that doesn't mean I want the organizing committees to crush them. I don't like that they're sequestering the new tech they have developed and trialed; I also wouldn't like that the organizing committees appropriate it. But we can discuss the intractability of such problems another time. It is possible, of course, that the settlement has nothing to do with this. We did look into Strevan's life, if in a somewhat cursory fashion, when we thought we were investigating a disappearance rather than a motive for murder, and nothing suggestive appeared." She paused, and scrunched her nose. "Although I must admit, I can imagine any number of murders being committed by the denizens and associates of that unaccountable club."

I shuddered. "Including the cats."

"As you say. Nonetheless, the Investigators looked closely at everyone they could find there, and found no indications; a vacuum, as it were, of solid narratives. The hidden platform, and the passions around it, neatly fits in that absence. But in what way?"

"It certainly seems," I proceeded with care, "that Elemaya had neither opportunity nor the inclination to kill Strevan."

"That was my strong impression," Mossa agreed. "We will of course confirm the story about the transportation constraints—" I noted a certain glee to her expression that made me suspect the confirmation would involve some personal experimentation with leaping onto railcars— "but for the moment, we will look for alternatives. So: What about that settlement might have caused someone to kill?"

"To keep it secret."

"Ye-e-es," Mossa said. "They might. But . . . surely they must know that they cannot keep it secret much longer?"

"They've done fairly well already."

"True but . . . they did not, notice, impose any obstacle on our departure."

They hadn't, though I shivered again remembering the ominous crowd watching us go. I had a sudden prickle of unease: Might they have damaged our railcar while we were enclosed with Elemaya, listening to her long-winded diatribes?

"The people who live on the platform might even welcome a dramatic conflict over its existence," Mossa went on blithely, while I shifted on the upholstery, listening for any falter in the engine or gyroscopes. "Insofar as that would let them yell about the strictures of the authorities to a wider audience. And they are far enough from the reaches of society that anything other than direct action by the organizing committees is unlikely to affect them much. However." She waited for me to catch up.

"Someone with an interest in the settlement, but who doesn't live there?" I asked belatedly. It was an intriguing enough idea to distract me from potential sabotage. "Someone providing them with assistance!"

"Mmm." Mossa looked thoughtful. "I wonder if it is framed that way. But I imagine, also, receiving some benefit in return."

"Or," I said, for my intellect was finally, it seemed, working as requested, "someone who was somehow compromised into engagement with the platform early on, and now can't extricate without risking scandal or repercussions."

"Precisely!" Mossa pointed at me. "Some combination of profit and compromise, someone with a lot to lose, and against that place the ambitious student, never enough resources, never taken quite seriously enough, encouraged to join the settlement but not truly believing in it . . ."

"Blackmail, extortion, something of the sort," I said.

"And the person Strevan would have attempted this on?"

I had to think, but not for long. "The bursar. The bursar of the Speculative faculty." I got a full smile for that one. "He has access to money—ahhh *stars*! Vecho Zei *told* me there was something going on over there, and I didn't fully attend."

"You attended enough to follow up on that thread," Mossa responded severely, "which brought us, indirectly I suppose but nonetheless, to Strevan's body and eventually to where we are now. *If* I may continue without further self-recriminations: has access to money." She counted on her fingers. "Is a Cat Club emeritus member, did you know? *And* was the person who opened, and later closed, the accusations of theft and embezzlement against Lup."

"Oh. Well then." I grinned at her. "Seems like an eminently plausible narrative to me."

We were silent for some time. My mind wandered to the apprehension of the bursar, shied away from the logistical difficulties involved, and leapt farther ahead. "What will happen to him?" Giant does not have prisons, as such. Instituting one on a separate platform is not as practical as it may initially seem—no one, to take just one problem, wants to give anyone an incentive to force their way into control of a railcar—and in any case free movement on the planet is a strong and cherished principle. Moreover, Classical evidence is vastly against the practice. "He won't be allowed near students again, that is certain, but . . ." Most people who committed crimes of trust lost their positions; they generally turned to agriculture, something that I, having grown up on an agricultural platform, had complicated feelings about. But for the perpetrator of a violent crime, there were a number of options, none of them perfect.

"He will have to atone to Strevan's father at least. Practically, that is likely to mean removal to Io."

I winced sinquerer. From the wry edge to Mossa's expression the movement had not gone unseen, and I hastened to explain. "I can't imagine facing that poor man." Let alone—what would he have to do to atone? Work for him?

"It is the least he can do," Mossa said, unconcerned about the fate of the bursar. Whether she had believed that I was no longer horrified by the mere idea of exile to Io I wasn't certain; but then, I wasn't certain whether I believed it myself.

It was dark outside the windows, still or again. I realized that I didn't even know which diurnal it was, whether I was supposed to be awake or asleep. That realization brought exhaustion, sudden and comprehensive. I excused myself to the washroom; when I came back, Mossa slipped past, already in her nightclothes, and both the benches had been unfolded into beds, while the storyboard cards gleamed still on the wall.

"Er, Mossa," I said when she returned, and almost had to close my eyes from the embarrassment of it. "That is . . . there's no need of keeping watch now, is there? I know the beds are narrow, but . . . surely we can manage?"

"Surely we can," she agreed. *As easy as that,* I thought. *I should ask for what I want . . . if only I could be sure, always, what it was.* And then Mossa had extinguished the light and, illuminated only by the faint azure refulgence of the fires in the grates below our beds, was slipping into the bunk where I lay. She was warm, and the narrowness constrained us to closeness, and my intellect immolated like silk.

Chapter 29

I woke, embarrassingly, from a violent nightmare in which I tried and failed, for the millionth time, to stop a deranged Modern geographer from slamming a wrench into Mossa's face. The calm of the quiescent railcar, with its gentle sway of motion, was disorienting, then reassuring, and Mossa was patting me in gentle, repeated cadences.

I didn't know what retribution Mossa had asked for against the man who had broken the bones in her face, or what had been granted. Perhaps she had asked for nothing at all, although given the violence of his actions and the desperation of his ravings the tribunal was likely to have required some combination of counseling, guarantee, and what was called "societal retribution" but was in all honesty largely punitive in significance.

It did seem to me a cruel quirk of our justice system

that I, not physically injured by the man, had not had a voice in his evaluation; and yet, he continued to haunt my dreams.

We passed the days of the journey quietly, staring from the window or reading. I managed a bit of work; Mossa, I believe, composed her report. We continued sharing the limited bed, and each night I knew we were closer to the last.

"You know," I said once, as the diurnals compounded into days, "that edge of independence that Lup and the rest display would have been much admired in some times and places." I had been thinking that Mossa's reaction to the group seemed unusually sharp, particularly for her.

She grasped immediately what I was asking, of course, although she took a few moments in what I imagined was the process of translating her reactions into words. "I dislike self-delusion. I particularly dislike when one or a few people's chosen delusion is powerful enough to draw in others. And the idolization of the settlers for what they could not avoid as opposed to for their choices, the donkulous invention of obstacles to try to achieve the same status . . ." She shook her head, breathed, then continued in a slower tone. "But all that included, I confess that perhaps . . . perhaps I do feel some excess ire towards them because in some ways I envy that very independence."

My innards contracted: Did she not want a relationship of affection, at all?

Thankfully, she went on; hopefully, without noticing my distress. "I find that, as loose as they are for me, the strictures of working for the Investigators do sometimes grate."

Relief made me hopeful. "Perhaps you can find another way of it."

She gave me a half smile, dazzling in the dim railcar. "Perhaps we can think of one together."

I woke one morning to Mossa shaking my shoulder. "Pleiti. Pleiti." She was dressed, and looked as though she had been for some time.

I sat up quickly and rubbed my face. "Where are we?"

"In a siding off Trubrant. We'll arrive in a few hours, and I wanted to make sure you were well alert."

"I hadn't realized how close we were!"

"You slept through a diurnal and a half, and not for the first time."

"Urgh." I rubbed my face.

She flashed me a partial smile. "You had been short of sleep for some time before that."

"I had lost track," I said, yawning.

Mossa handed me a cup and waited until I was more focused to proceed. "Pleiti, we should have a strategy to deal with the bursar." (She used his name but I find, in writing this account, that I prefer not to. *Evil men are ceded importance,* et cetera.)

"Arrest him, surely."

"Ideally, yes, but please keep in mind that he's dangerous." I raised my eyebrows, a rather silly reaction to the reminder that a literal murderer might be dangerous. "Leaving aside the *actual murder*," Mossa said with some asperity, "he's already tried to kill you once. The library panel?" she added, since I apparently looked as blank as I felt.

Somehow, it was harder to brush it off as an accident when I could imagine a specific person creeping around the Silvered, sawing at metalwork.

"His suspicions were already aroused; he will have noticed our absence and drawn his conclusions. I would like you to wait in your rooms while I pursue him, but I must admit I'm a little concerned they may be snared."

"Oh, *really*!"

"He's a university official, you know. It would not be hard for him to gain access."

I subsided, recalling my interview with the man: he had been behind his desk the whole time, but I remembered the crackle of irritability that could have been defensive anger, his obvious physicality. "How is it that in both these cases the wrongdoer has belonged to the university?"

Mossa shot me a sympathetic look. "I don't suppose I could convince you to disembark here, or at Prupal"—the next platform to Valdegeld—"until it's over?"

"He's going to be after you at least as much as after me!" I retorted. "Why don't you sit it out?"

That, she was clearly not willing to do.

"Very well," she grumped, after an interval of somewhat volatile discussion. "We will both get off in Valdegeld and then we will stay together, agreed?" I nodded, with only the least show of reluctance to convince her; in truth, I had no wish to be worrying about her meeting a potential confrontation without me.

"Can the Investigators help?"

Mossa scowled but agreed: "Yes, I suppose that must be our first stop. We will make for the bureau, gather our forces, and—I do worry, though, that if he's watching the station that will just give him time to scarper."

"If he's watching the station, ready to run, he will get away before we get to his office in any case. Why don't we wire the bureau from here?" I asked finally, confused as to why Mossa hadn't thought of it. "They can meet us near his office, or near the station if you really think he'll be waiting there."

Mossa grumbled some more at that; I gathered that there were some interoffice politics at stake and also, perhaps, glory. This seemed silly to me—rather pleasing to be the more practical one, for once—and after confirming that it probably wouldn't make us miss our next window between railcars, she agreed to go find the telegraph office in the Trubrant station.

As she opened the door I felt a sudden misgiving. "What if he knows we're here?" We had been stopped on the siding for some time. "I'll go with you."

"Hardly likely, Pleiti. Even if he somehow learned of our arrival on the instant, he still wouldn't have had time to get here from Valdegeld."

"But," I started, though I really had nothing to follow it up with.

"Oh, very well, come along then. Probably do us both good to stretch our legs. And you can get us some hot food while I write the wire, they do a very good pissaladière at one of the stalls here."

Nothing untoward occurred in the station, which didn't stop me from feeling a distinct sense of relief when the railcar doors had closed behind us again. Of course we hadn't time to wait for a response to the telegram, so we pulled into Valdegeld Main Station without any surety that backup had been allocated. Remembering the respectful awe I'd seen Valdegeld Investigators show Mossa, I was inclined to trust that they'd taken her request seriously; Mossa, however, reminded me ominously that the Valdegeld Bureau staffed only three Investigators, and they might well have other priorities.

We stepped down from the railcar on the empty private andén, therefore, with sharp attention toward anyone who might be waiting for us, threatening or benign.

Then we stepped out into the hall of the main station and stopped, both of us, in the face of crowds and chaos, elaborate bunting and cacophony, festive scents and a profusion of suspended shimmer. It was the Feast-Day of Valdegeld.

Chapter 30

We could be forgiven for forgetting about the occurrence of the festival. (I say *we*; Mossa claims that she had not forgotten, merely did not realize quite how exuberant the celebration would be, but this is evident nonsense). (Classical) centuries into the settlement on Giant, the measuring of time continued to vary between Classical intervals, which were accustomed but no longer linked to any orbital reality, and the ungainly markers of Giant's rotation and revolution: short days, extremely long years. Anniversaries and other such celebrations, such as this one commemorating the fixing of Valdegeld's proto-platform onto its ring, were worked out in a complicated compromise. Moreover, our (or at least my) sense of time had been thrown off by the long journey and the haphazardness of our schedule.

In any case, we arrived in the thick of it. Eager group-ings of merrymakers from other platforms were disem-barking en masse, filling the station; a glance through the Avenue Supal exit told me that august street was thronged and pulsing. "We can take the Vennikam exit," I called to Mossa over my shoulder, and I saw her nod grimly be-fore I turned to edge through the swirling fog of festival-goers. A moment later her preoccupied expression clicked a realization for me: the Investigators would be entirely occupied by the celebrations. We couldn't hope for their assistance; it was hard to imagine they had even received our wire.

Vennikam was a narrow alley that debouched onto the considerably larger Larkavery Way. That street was nearly as crowded as Supal, but at least the crowd was mostly Valdeans, with few extra-platformers gawping at the ar-chitecture and the light fixtures. I was going to ask where we were aiming, but Mossa had already set off through the multitude in the direction of the Speculative Campus.

We had edged past the applause section for a Classi-cal go-go performance, struggled through the queue for a stall selling (an undoubtedly diluted version of) univer-sity scones, and threaded around a chess tourney when I realized we had veered somewhat from the most direct route to the bursar's office. I caught at Mossa's elbow to point this out; she leaned toward me before I had even spoken and called out, "He won't be at work, lives on Strassvar." I was nodding (and wondering just how early she had suspected him, to have found out where he lived) when her eyes caught on something behind me. Before I could react she had yanked me around, stepped in, put her fragile body between me and the monumental figure of the bursar hurtling towards us on momentum and fury.

I am embarrassed to admit it now, but I yelled "Duck!" It was so like my nightmare, my memory, my desperate desire to relive that moment and tell her something useful instead of shouting her name like a fool—fortunately, it did not matter, as the noise of the festival around us engulfed my shout and I'm certain no one heard it. Mossa, thankfully, was entirely concentrated on the task before her.

I saw her hand move toward the whip-lasso at her waist and then jerk to a stop: that weapon would be dangerous, as well as unwieldy, in the crowd. It was only a moment's misthought, but it very nearly cost her: the bursar was as set in his trajectory as a meteor, teeth bared, and I saw the brilliance of a pointed blade in his raised arm. But Mossa was exceedingly nimble; she slipped through the arc of the weapon and whirled immediately to face him again. He pivoted, panting—he must have been hurrying for some time to catch up to us—had he been waiting for us at the station?—and circled, searching for advantage. Mossa feinted, then jabbed, and I saw that she was holding the small knife she had brandished at the memorial, so long ago. She stabbed again but in the critical moment she was jostled from the side by someone hurrying to take a turn at the miniature ring-races set up along the side of the road, and the bursar closed in again.

Do not imagine that during all this I gawped immobile,

as artificially impotent as a woman in a Classical film. As soon as Mossa had dodged the first time I looked around for something, anything of use. A gleam caught my eye, and I darted at the stall of a vendor, grabbed a toy railcar as long as my forearm, fashioned from metal and with pleasing heft. I swung round again to see Mossa being bumped and stumbling. The currents had shifted around me; the throng had realized something unusual was occurring, although I'd wager most of them thought it was a performance rather than in earnest. Those nearest the fight were turning inward, and I had to shove through them to get close enough, but that meant the bursar didn't see me as he trundled towards Mossa, arm raised again. When I swung the model railcar backhand up into his face, it must have come as a complete surprise.

Mossa was on him before I could hit a second time, taking advantage of the gap left by the startled crowd to lash his arms with the whip-lasso, showing him her small knife at very close range when he spat and shrieked. "Thank you, Pleiti," she said, as she turned him in the direction she wanted to go and set out at a steady shove.

"Truly my pleasure," I said, and it was. The solid reverberations of that thump had been immensely satisfying.

Chapter 31

I followed Mossa to the Investigators' office, occasionally stepping in front to run interference when the festival crowd got particularly thick. There was, as I had suspected, no one there but the porter, and our telegram was lying still in its envelope on the mail tray. However, the porter gripped the situation within a few words from Mossa, and was well capable of assisting us with what we needed. Once the bursar was prevented from threatening further harm, Mossa settled in to the paperwork. I offered to assist, but she either saw my reluctance or deduced that I wouldn't be much help anyway, and asked only that I stop around the corner to get her a curry, full spice, before waving me home.

I trudged through the festival, head aching, berating myself for being so exhausted when I had done little but sleep and read (and dally) for the past week. Only when I came in sight of my own arched entryway and felt my heart leap did I realize that my yearning was not for physical rest but for the emotional soulagement of being quietly in my own place and alone. I sprang up the stairs with renewed energy, bathed for an extended period, donned my favorite dressing gown, and ordered laksa.

In the magnificent serenity of postprandial tea, I wondered how Mossa was getting on; there was surely quite a bit to untangle, and I suspected the eventual return of the Investigators would only further complicate things. I felt a fissure of doubt: Would she not come back to my rooms when she was done? After all, she too must be longing for her own space; perhaps she would return directly to Sembla and I would see her the next time she came?

I told myself that would be understandable and, more than that, endurable, but I moved my tea to the side table by the window seat and resisted the lure of my smooth sheets and cool pillow, waiting until, with relief, I made out Mossa's figure turning down my street at last.

We did not talk about the aftermath until the next day—or rather, until after we had both slept for many hours consecutively, since we had lost track of diurnals. I had gone out to get breakfast from the poultry farm: spiced eggs cocotte, shredded yucca with garlic, and something they called coffee, although I had it on good authority from a culinary scholar that the plant they were using was entirely different from that referred to in Classical sources. We did not speak of the case until we were relaxing in a pleasant sated haze before the fire.

"He refused to confess to Strevan's murder," Mossa told me. "But it didn't matter; the knife he attacked me with was what cut Strevan's throat, they're sure of it." She had her foot wrapped and hoisted on a hassock; she had twisted her ankle when she stumbled during the fight, and although it was not badly injured we were both eager to coddle and be coddled.

I leaned my head back against her good knee, feeling the heat from the fire on my legs. "And then? Did he explain about the blackmail once they had him?"

"Mmph. Obstreperous all the way. I was able to bluff him into admitting that he knew about Little Worth"—the sardonic name she was using for the platform on the other side of the planet—"and that they had gotten funding and resources from the Speculative faculty"—I winced, imagining the repercussions—"but he claimed that it was all embezzled or stolen, blamed Lup as a 'bad influence,' said she corrupted all his student staff. It won't hold up," she added, registering my concern.

I sighed extravagantly. "Why, why is the malfeasant always part of the university?"

Mossa glanced down at me obliquely, perhaps wondering to what degree I was joking. "I would say your sample size is small," she pointed out mildly. "But beyond that . . ."

Beyond that, the university was powerful, and sheltered powerful people, and not all of them were pure of purpose or temptation-resistant.

"I hope at least this won't cause you further distress." She let her hand drift into my hair. "I know that the reactions to—to what happened with the rector have been difficult for you."

"Ahh, I'm getting over it. And while it's early days yet, I think this will be different." I had spent some time in the common room that morning, while Mossa, for once, was still sleeping. Despite or perhaps because of the festival, the news about the bursar's crimes had spread more quickly than I had imagined, but unlike the startled awe following the situation with the rector, I had detected an only slightly muted glee. The bursar had less power or (perhaps as a consequence of lacking the first) charisma or popularity than Rector Spandal, and his felonies were more comprehensible. The few people who had spoken to me directly about it, in fact, seemed rather impressed with my role. Puncturing one university muckamuck was suspect; dismantling the reputations of two was, apparently, an indication that I was on the side of justice.

Wanting to change the subject (and wanting to know), I stretched my legs out and asked as casually as I could, "Are you staying around?"

Mossa yawned. "I should get back to Sembla, make a personal report there. And air out my flat as well. My leg should be well enough by tomorrow." She looked down at me, eyelashes lowered. "If it's not inconvenient, I thought perhaps I'd come back on the weekend."

"Not inconvenient at all," I said, as if joy weren't coursing through me. I cast about for something to concretize the plan. "Perhaps we could go to the opera."

"What's playing?"

I reached to the shelf on the wall and checked the laminate. "*Boys over Flowers*. The Tambunan libretto, not the Sato version."

Mossa made a mueca; she had never been fond of Classical melodrama. She held out her hand for the laminate and flipped through. "Let's wait a few weeks and go for *Infomocracy* instead."

I wrinkled my nose. "They simplify the book too much."

"Snob." There was so much affection in Mossa's tone that I felt a pulse of joy. "Besides, the melody for the gif montage scene is beautiful." She began to hum.

"As you like," I said carelessly. "Maybe a quiet weekend this time, then."

"You've certainly earned it." She said it softly, and I looked up, startled.

"Surely you don't think I resent any of these, these . . ." I tried to think of a non-judgmental term. "These adventures you've, er, included me in?" I narrowly avoided saying *dragged me on,* and from Mossa's expression I thought she knew it.

"I took you away from your work on two long journeys, including on a shuttle journey which you *hated,* wasted days of your time going to that ridiculous settlement, put you in danger from falling libraries and knife-wielding bursars—"

"Mossa!" I stopped her, laughing. "Truly, it was extraordinary." She looked skeptical, and I sighed and went point by point. "Our experiences have influenced how I work, for the better. I am grateful to have gone back to Io and seen more of it, even if I did hate the process of getting there; I would *never* call that time in the railcar a waste, even aside from the fact that I've gotten detailed notes for a monograph out of it; er, what was the other thing? Oh yes, the danger. Well. A little danger is salutary, I think. A tonic."

Mossa chuckled, somewhat mollified. "As you say, Pleiti. I certainly find your assistance invaluable, I am glad to hear it is not such a sacrifice."

"Certainly not. In fact," I was coasting on the potent glow of being invaluable, of Mossa worrying about my well-being, of the easy sense of understanding, "I'm hoping these experiences will help me develop better ways of doing my research." I looked up at her beloved face. "I just have to keep at it."

Acknowledgments

Enormous thanks to everyone who read, enjoyed, talked about, reviewed, or otherwise supported *The Mimicking of Known Successes;* I am so happy to continue exploring Mossa and Pleiti's world with this book. Thank you to all the communities of friends, real life and virtual, that support me with friendship and assistance and advice and understanding. I'm grateful for public schools, public libraries, public parks, public playgrounds, public transportation, public beaches, public sanitation, public broadcasting, and public plazas. Thank you to my beta readers, Dora Vázquez Older, Carmen Crow Sheehan, Annahita de la Mare, and especially Charlie Jane Anders, for some very useful comments. Enormous thanks to Brent Lambert, who made this book much better with his careful reading, constructive suggestions, and overall editing. Thanks to everyone at Tordotcom who helped turn this story into a book and get it to the people who would want to read it, with extra thanks to Christine Foltzer for the gorgeous cover:

Editorial:
Eli Goldman

Publicists:
Saraciea Fennell
Jocelyn Bright

Marketer:
Samantha Friedlander

Art Director & Jacket Designer:
Christine Foltzer

Production Editor:
Lauren Hougen

Production Manager:
Jim Kapp

Interior Designer:
Greg Collins

Copyeditor:
Christina MacDonald

Proofreader:
Andrea Wilk

Cold Reader:
Jaime Herbeck

And always thank you to my family: Dora, Marc, Daniel, Britt, Amari, Lou, Calyx, Paz, Azul.